In The Beginning:

Thirty Points Where the Bible and the Hard Sciences Tell the Same Story of Origins

My journey of discovering the science of divine creation.

By Kenneth M. Goss

Table of Contents

Dedication

This book is dedicated to my family for whom it was written. I pray that each one, for generations to come, will recognize God as their creator and live their lives accordingly.

Acknowledgements

I am grateful to several friends and family members who have helped with proofreading and other inputs. I suppose no book is ever totally a one-man show, and mine is no different. I also owe much to a long list of authors, pastors, and teachers who have shaped my understanding of both science and scripture.

Preface

I am the product of a public high school education with a liberal dose of emphasis on evolution, but I am also the product of a fundamental Christian church background and a Christian college. I once heard a famous preacher say that when he was young, he had a drug problem. He was drug to church every time the doors were open. That pretty much describes my youth as well.

So, with that background, I am very aware of the conflict between Darwinism (evolution), which claims to be settled science, and scripture, which claims to be the word of a supernatural being that we commonly refer to as God. One says that everything originated through totally materialistic natural causes (no God required), and the other says that everything originated from the will, the intellect, and the power of an eternal, supernatural, almighty God. That conflict has been brewing for well over 100 years, maybe over 200 years.

In our public schools, we are taught that everything developed or evolved naturally, accidentally, with no cause; therefore, there is no need for a Creator God. In our churches, we are taught that the Bible says God created everything from nothing. Does the conflict between these two positions challenge your faith? What if I could demonstrate that the true hard Sciences and the Bible tell the same story of origins? What if there is no conflict between true science and Scripture?

Like me, many people have had a conflict in their minds. They want to believe in creation as outlined in scripture, and they will give lip service to it, but deep inside, they have some level of conflict or doubt because of what they have been taught in church compared to what they have heard from an education system and a media that presumes natural Darwinian evolution is a proven fact. I will attempt to resolve that conflict.

Folks use several mind games or concepts to try to resolve the conflict. In Chapter Seven, I outline several common concepts that try to reconcile what is perceived as divine creation in six days about 6000 years ago with science, which we are taught has proven billions of years of history in the universe. None of them fully satisfied me, so I started a search for an answer.

Some folks will read this book and ask, "What is the point? I believe in the Creator God, and that is all I need." However, what do you say to a skeptic? In 1 Peter 3:15, we are told to be always ready to give a reason for the hope that is in us. For me, the materials in this book are a strong reason for my faith that there is a God and He is the creator of all things, just as the Bible says.

Introduction

The Judeo-Christian Scriptures give creation prominence, making it the first 10 words of the Bible. Gen 1:1 says, "In the beginning God created the heavens and the earth." If it was the first thing God wanted to communicate to man, maybe we should give it careful attention. What is more, some 27 books of the Bible contain over 100 verses referencing God as the creator or maker of everything. If it is repeated so many times, maybe we should give it more attention.

Given that experts on both sides of the creation vs science debate have very hard, dogmatic positions which seem to be miles apart, it may surprise you to know that my thesis or theme for this book is that Biblical Creation and the findings of science both tell the same story of origins/creation. Just as two witnesses can observe the same event, then use different words and different emphasis to relate what may sound like different accounts, Scripture and science use different words and different emphasis to describe the same events in the same sequence. If you wade through the dogmas and ideologies, the two stories can be understood in a way that reconciles the conflict between Scripture and science. If understood correctly, there is no conflict. How am I going to show that? I have identified 30 key points where the two stories converge. With 30 points of agreement, the odds are over 1 billion to one that they are the same story, even if the words used to tell that story are different.

Many books have been written by learned men with PHD degrees in some branch of science showing that for one reason or another, both the concept of Darwinian natural evolution and the concept of spontaneous generation of first life by totally natural chemical actions as taught by its proponents today are not feasible, not probable, not reasonable, not rational, not logical, not possible, and so on. Those books conclude that some form of supernatural divine action is required to create the universe and all life. However, they often fail to follow up and show how the account of creation in the Bible is true and accurate. I will focus on the scientific accuracy of the Biblical story of creation.

My objective is not to shake the foundations of the faithful or to convert the faithful to my interpretation of Genesis. If you have a firm belief in any interpretation of Genesis that leads you to a firm faith in the Creator God, hang on to that faith.

My goal is to reach those people with doubts about God because of what they believe to be a creation myth. If I can show that the account of creation in the Bible is scientifically solid, that it is not a myth, then a barrier to belief in a Creator God will be breached and a bridge to faith will be built.

Chapter 1:
Why Study Creation?

Why is it important to study the creation story in the Bible?

First, it is important because the story of creation in Genesis is the foundation for all Judeo-Christian beliefs. The first five words of Genesis say, "In the beginning God created." The truth expressed in those five words introduces us to the God who is the subject of the rest of the Bible and establishes the basis for His authority.

For a long time, I missed or overlooked the significance of God being the creator. Then I recognized that any creator of anything has full authority to make their creation whatever they please. If I am creating a sculpture, or a painting, or a musical score, or a literary work, or a video game, or an automobile, or a skyscraper, or a toaster, or anything else, as the creator I have the authority to make it whatever I want it to be and to make it function any way I want it to function. As the creator of the universe and all life in it, God has full legal and moral authority to make it according to His wishes and to demand that it function according to His wishes.

As creator, God gets to set the rules. Those rules include the laws of physics that govern the behavior of inanimate forces and materials. Those rules include the instincts programmed into most of the animal kingdom. Those rules also include the moral laws given to humans to govern their relationships with God and with each other.

Whichever rules they may be, God has the sole authority to set them. He has the ultimate, absolute, total authority. Just in case that doesn't sink in, let me say that when someone with that kind of authority says "jump," you need to ask how high on your way up, after your feet have left the ground.

Without a Creator God, there would be no authority to establish any moral code. We say it is wrong to steal because God said it is wrong to steal. We say it is wrong to lie because God said it is wrong to lie. There is a long list of things we say are wrong because God says they are wrong, and things that we say are noble and right because God says they are noble and right. Without a moral code, there is no such thing as sin and no need for a savior. With no authoritative moral code, what you get is moral chaos.

God considers it so important to recognize Him as Creator that He made it one of the Ten Commandments. The fourth commandment (Exodus 20:8-11) says we are to work six days and set aside the seventh day to honor God **because** God set aside the seventh day of creation as a day of rest. So, any time we observe a seven-day week with one day of rest, we are recognizing that God created the universe in six divine workdays and rested on the seventh day. This commandment is so important to God that He condemned Israel often for failing to keep the seventh day holy or set apart. So here is a challenge: do you keep one day of the seven holy and set aside to honor God?

Second, it is important to study creation so that you can be fully convinced of the existence of a Creator with moral authority to guide your life. In today's culture, we have been taught for over 100 years (four or five generations) that Darwinian evolution by natural causes is the source of our existence. No God required. We are nothing more than highly evolved animals. People who believe they are mere animals will soon start to act like animals.

Third, it is important to study creation because what you believe about creation and the Creator God has a tremendous impact on your worldview and your life. When we teach our youth for a hundred years (4 or 5 generations) that they are nothing more than highly evolved animals, we should not be surprised when they act like animals.

People whose worldview is rooted in Darwinian evolution are capable of racism, genocide, and many other forms of cruelty. The Nazis, the communists, the Khmer Rouge, and other infamous groups have been heavily influenced by concepts of natural evolution and survival of the fittest. They have murdered millions of people whom they considered unfit to survive. The Darwinists of today tend to ignore that history.

If your worldview is based on Darwinian evolution, you are likely to accept abortion, infanticide, genocide, suicide, euthanasia, and much more. After all, if we are merely animals with no immortal soul, then what could be wrong with killing old folks, unwanted babies, and racial groups that we consider to be burdensome or undesirable? If they are offensive to us, or a burden to us, or unprofitable to us, then get rid of them. After all, they are only animals. Such is Darwinian reasoning.

As an engineer, I am trained to look for the root causes of problems. If my engine fails, I ask why. Because it lacked lubrication. Why did it lack lube? Because the oil pump was not pumping oil. Why was it not pumping oil? Because it was plugged with sludge. Why was it plugged? And so the search continues for the root cause of the problem.

Today, we see a lot of people acting like animals. They are totally self-serving. They take what they want in order to satisfy their desires for food, shelter, sexual gratification, and so on without regard for any moral code. They are willing to use violence to get what they want. They have no regard for truth, compassion, love, civility, grace, mercy, or any of the higher qualities of humanity. In short, we have moral chaos. Why? What is the root cause? For over 100 years, our public schools have been teaching that man is no more than a highly developed animal. Either directly or by default, they teach that there is no such thing as God. He is only a myth. No Creator God = No absolute standards = moral chaos.

On the other hand, if you believe and accept that there is a Creator God who has established rules of behavior, you will develop what is often called the higher principles of civility. Honesty, integrity, respect for life, kindness, and many social graces are a direct result of following God's direction for your life. Accepting the direction of the Creator God also develops peace, joy, and other positive internal qualities.

Fourth, it is important to study creation because God says it is important. God is referred to as the creator or maker of all things over 100 times in the Bible. Those references occur in nearly half of the books of the Bible. If God said it that many times, He must consider it important. If He considers it to be important, maybe we should also consider it to be important.

Fifth, it is important to study creation because of the awe factor. If there is no awe for God, there can really be no worship. The awesomeness of God starts with the awesomeness of His creation. When you look at and study the natural world, if you believe that God is the creator, you can't help but be filled with a sense of awe for the creator of that world. A popular hymn starts with "O Lord my God, when I in awesome wonder consider all the worlds Thy hands have made." It goes on to say, "How great Thou art."

Whether you are looking at the countless stars in the heavens or looking at a microscopic creature, the awesomeness of the creator is unmistakable. Whether you are looking at a magnificent mountain or the endless expanse of the oceans, the awesomeness of the creator is on display. Wherever you look in the natural world, you see the handiwork of an awesome God.

Then, if you consider the love that this awesome God has shown toward you, it is almost beyond imagination that the awesome Creator God cares for me. Now you can have a true sense of worship.

Chapter 2:
The Creator God

At some point in my creation journey of discovery, I began to see a truth that I had not seen before. Why is the story of creation set in the first chapter of the Bible?

The first 10 words of the Bible in the English Language are "In the Beginning God created the heavens and the earth." These are the first 10 words because they set the foundation for all Judeo-Christian beliefs. The 10 words of this first verse of the Bible are arguably the most important words of the 31,102 verses in the Bible. These 10 words introduce us to the Creator God that we are to worship. They teach us a lot about God:

- God is eternal. He existed before the universe existed, so he transcends time. He had no beginning. He has always existed. Time is irrelevant and immaterial to Him. The universe has a beginning, but God, the creator of the universe, does not. He is eternal.

- God is omniscient or all-knowing. He is the supreme intellect. No one is smarter than He is. His mind conceived the complexities, the precision, the beauty, the function, etc. of the universe. His mind created everything from the most immense galaxies to the most minute single-cell creatures, and He did this using only 17 subatomic particles and 4 basic forces (see chapter 9). Imagine if you were given 17 sizes of Lego bricks and 4 kinds of glue and you had to create a fully functioning major city with skyscrapers and energy grids, and streets, and sewer systems, and so on. This is only mildly analogous to what God did in His creation.

- God is omnipotent or all-powerful. He is the supreme power or force. No one has more power than He has. He supplied the power/energy to make every particle in our universe. Also, His power holds it all together. If splitting the atoms in a few pounds of uranium makes an atomic bomb with enough energy to destroy a city, imagine the immense energy required to create all of the trillions of trillions of trillions of tons of atoms in the universe.

- God is the reason we exist. We and the universe around us were created because He willed it to happen. He created us and the universe we live in because He wanted to. He spoke and the worlds came into being. All things happen by His will and for His purposes.

- God is the supreme authority. As creator, He alone has the authority to make the universe function in any way He pleases. We often miss the significance of God being the creator. It bears repeating that the creator of anything, a painting, a song, a sculpture, an engineered structure, etc., has the full authority and right to make it any way he wants to make it and make it function any way he wants to make it function. As creator, God gets to set the rules. As I said before, these rules include the laws of physics that determine the behavior of inanimate objects. They also include the instincts that are programmed into the animal world. They also include the moral laws given to mankind to show us how we are to function, that is, how we are to relate to God and to each other. Without this Creator God, who has supreme moral authority, there would be no definition of right and wrong. There would be no authoritative standard. There would be no definition of sin. Without God's laws, there would be moral chaos.

The rest of the story of creation builds on these first 10 words. It gives us details in a broad outline to show us the truth of those first 10 words. In fact, the rest of the Bible builds on these first 10 words, teaching us about this supreme being that we call God.

Amazingly, these simple 10 words have spawned multiple interpretations (see chapter 7). I understand these first 10 words to be an introduction or summary statement. You can almost imagine it saying, "In the beginning God created the heavens and the earth… details to follow." Furthermore, I tend to believe that the reference to "heavens" and "earth" refers to the spirit realm and the physical realm as opposed to the universe and planet Earth, the third rock from the sun.

Because we can't see it, smell it, or touch it, we often overlook the spirit realm. However, it exists, and it too was created by the same God who created our physical realm. So, maybe those first 10 words could be paraphrased as: "In the beginning God created the spirit realm (or the angelic realm) and the physical realm… details to follow."

This Creator God is the God that the Bible teaches us to fear, reverence, respect, worship, serve, obey, love, etc. If this God is a fake or a myth, then millions of people over thousands of years have been duped. However, the testimonies of millions of those people confirm that God is not a fake or a myth. He has had a profound impact on millions of lives.

As we will see, the story of creation has been confirmed by the findings of science. This alone should prove beyond any doubt that this God is real. If the story of creation in the Bible gives us the same series of events in the same sequence as what science has identified in its studies of origins, then the Biblical story of creation is verified to be scientifically and historically accurate.

From this, we can deduce that the God of creation is real. He is not a myth like Santa Claus or the Easter Bunny. If, or since, He is very real, then this God with the supreme power, intellect, and authority is not someone with whom you should trifle. You may be able to ignore Him for a while, but eventually you will no longer be able to ignore Him. You will have to deal with Him. You will have to face Him. Are you ready?

Chapter 3:
God's word / God's world

Why, you might ask, do I believe that the story of creation in the Bible and the story of origins told by science actually tell the same story? After all, on the surface, they seem to be very different stories.

The simple answer is that they MUST tell the same story. If (since) there is a God, and if (since) that God created the universe, and if (since) that God inspired the writing of the Holy Scriptures/God's Word, then that God is revealed to us through two sources. First, He is revealed to us by His Word, and second, He is revealed to us through the worlds that He created.

Science is the study/observation of the natural universe, or the worlds God created. So, an unbiased study of nature will reveal to us the same God who inspired the writing of His Word, the Bible. In Psalm 19:1, the Bible says that "the heavens declare the glory of God." The same God who inspired the scriptures is revealed in the creation.

Note that Darwinian evolution is not true science. When I say "science," I am referring to the hard sciences, which include disciplines in the physical sciences like Physics, chemistry, and astronomy, which are characterized by rigor, objectivity, and precision in their methods. The speculations of Darwinian atheistic philosophy do not qualify since they cannot be tested or mathematically modeled. In fact, the true hard sciences consistently debunk the basic tenets of evolutionary theory.

In Romans 1:20, Paul tells us that the invisible character of God can be clearly seen in His creation, so even men who have not had the scriptures available to them are without any excuse for not knowing God. So, God is revealed to men through His creation.

As early as Galileo, and probably earlier, men have recognized two sources of revelation about God. One is His inspired word, and the other is His created universe. It seems axiomatic that if we have two sources of revelation given by the same God about the same God, when we study His Word and study His world, what we learn from the two sources MUST agree.

Now then, I see three important points to be recognized. First, both science and scripture tell us that there was a progression of events that brought us to the universe we see today and all of the life forms in that universe. There is a sequence to those events, and that sequence tells us a story. If the sequence of events told by scripture and the sequence of events told by science are the same events in the same sequence, then **<u>Scripture and science tell the same story of origins (29).</u>**

Second, we need to recognize that the two stories are written to different audiences for different purposes. The story of creation in the Bible is written to common people living over 3000 years ago, people who had limited knowledge of science. The original audience was a group of nomadic people who had recently escaped years of slavery in Egypt, plus years of indoctrination in Egyptian culture and religion. The story of creation in the bible is written with the purpose of showing the audience that there is one supreme God who created everything, and He alone is worthy of their worship. None of the created things is worthy of worship. Only the Creator is worthy. The Biblical account of creation is a very broad outline story. On the other hand, the story of origins told by 21st-century scientists is written to fellow 21st-century scientists with the purpose of advancing the careers of those 21st-century scientists. It is a very detailed story.

Third, the two stories are written in different languages. The Bible story of creation is written in simple language that can be understood by all people. The story of origins told by science is written to modern-day men and especially to scientific scholars. It is often written in deeply technical language with technical terms that can only be fully understood by the scientific elite. It is written to impress their peers and advance their careers.

Also, the story of creation in the Bible was written in the Hebrew language as spoken some 3300 years ago. That language had a total vocabulary of about 8,000 words. The story of origins told by science today is written in 21st-century English, which has a vocabulary of over 170,000 words. For example, the ancient Hebrew language had no words for electricity, gravity, orbits, planets, atoms, and a lot of other words that we use regularly today. Without specific words for some of these features, the writers of the Bible had to describe creation events in word pictures that their audience would understand.

Of particular interest is the fact that ancient Hebrew had no word for what we today would call an era or an eon of time. We will discuss this more when we talk about the length of the days of creation. (see chapter 14)

Much of what any high school student today knows about science has only been discovered in the past few decades. New words develop as new discoveries are made. Modern science uses words that even today many of us have difficulty understanding.

So, while the two stories may sound different on the surface, as we dig deeper into them, we will find that they have many parallels. They tell the same story in different words, addressed to different audiences for different purposes, but they relate the same events in the same sequence. **<u>Scripture and science tell the same story of origins.</u>**

If I can show that these two stories converge on a common narrative, it will show that the story of creation in the bible is not a myth, as many claim. If the creation story is not a myth, then the Creator God of the Bible is also not a myth. If (since) God's written Word and God's created worlds tell us the same story about our origins, we should probably pay close attention to both the Bible and the creation. Are you studying God's Word?

Since God's Word and God's world both reveal the same God to us, if we study His Word and study His creation (science), and we come to conflicting conclusions, then one conclusion or the other needs to be adjusted. The words of scripture are true. The facts of nature are real. Only the conclusions drawn from those words and facts are subject to interpretation by men. Those conclusions may be subject to the biases and perspectives of men.

Aristotle said, "It is not the facts that divide men but the interpretation of the facts." If I may paraphrase a bit, it is not the words of Scripture that divide men, but the interpretations of the words. Also, it is not the data of science that divides men but the interpretation of that data.

Some people argue that there is no need to reconcile the Biblical account of creation with the findings of science because God's word is true, and we don't need to change it to agree with science. While that is a very pious-sounding statement, I am left to wonder if I am understanding God's word correctly or if I am understanding an interpretation made by well-educated and sincere but nonetheless limited and biased human scholars. Is there no room for learning better understandings of God's Word based on what we observe and measure in the universe He created? We don't need to change His word to agree with science, but we may need to adjust our understanding of His word. Of course, we may also need to adjust our interpretations of our observations of His created world to agree with the Scriptures.

For decades, Bible scholars have used the findings of archeologists to clarify the meanings of passages in Scripture. Those discoveries can help us understand what life was like in Biblical times and what certain expressions really mean. In a similar manner, the discoveries made by other scientists who are observing God's world can help us to better understand the story of creation.

The YEC folks claim that adjusting our understanding of the words of Scripture in order to fit what we observe in God's creation is a slippery slope that leads to wholesale changes in our understanding of Scripture. On the other hand, forcing an understanding of the words of Scripture that is in clear conflict with carefully observed data of the created world is a sharp cliff. At the bottom of that cliff are the ruined souls of people who could not accept the existence and authority of a Creator God because of a forced dogmatic misinterpretation of the words of scripture. When you insist on a creation done in 6 days of 24-hour duration in the face of clear physical evidence of a longer timeline, you erect an impenetrable barrier for persons seeking after God. You drive them away from a God whom they conclude is clearly a myth.

Chapter 4:
Basic concepts of origins

I grew up regularly attending a very independent fundamental Bible preaching church, and I went to a public high school. So, I got a good dose of two basic concepts of origins.

Today, there are still two basic concepts of origins. A materialistic concept believes that all things came about through purposeless natural causes, and the divine creation/Intelligent Design concept believes that an intelligent agent designed and built everything. The first is commonly called "evolution," even though it is more properly called "Darwinism" or "neo-Darwinism." The second is called divine creation or ID (Intelligent Design). Both look at the evidence we see in the universe and in the world around us, and they interpret that evidence in different ways to come to different conclusions.

Darwinism has evolved into an ideology with the fervor of a religion. Darwinism is the creation story of atheism. Contrary to what many believe, atheism is a religious belief. A belief that there exists no supernatural creator god with ultimate absolute authority defaults into worship of man as the ultimate authority. Since atheism is perceived by many to be non-religious or secular, and since the US Constitution has a law against the state establishing any state church, atheism is allowed, even demanded, in our public schools and in our government; in fact, it is the only "religion" allowed in the public domain. In spite of the constitutional provision against the state creating a church, atheism has become the de facto state religion of America and indeed much of the world.

This might be a good point to inject a definition. The term "science" is often misapplied. Science applies to disciplines that can be proven true by experiments and mathematics. Things like physics, chemistry, and astronomy can be described as science. In true science, theories are accepted as fact when they are proven by tests and measurements. On the other hand, things like geology, paleontology, and archeology deal with interpreting evidence to determine past events. Those events cannot be reproduced and proven by experiments and mathematics. These are more properly called natural philosophy. Theories are accepted as fact when a majority of experts in that field accept them.

For any person with an open mind, it is not too difficult to debunk the Darwinian atheistic concept of origins by totally natural causes. With the advances in science today, we know enough to prove pretty conclusively that natural causes are inadequate to explain our origins. Those who still cling to that concept do so for ideological (dare I say religious) reasons.

Recently, maybe the past 20 years, many books and articles have been written that question the efficacy of the Darwinian theory of natural causes. When Darwin first published his book on the origin of species in the mid-1800s, it sounded very reasonable. With the instruments of the day, a single cell looked like a blob of protoplasm with a skin around it. However, with the development of more powerful telescopes and microscopes, plus the tremendous advances in our understanding of science, in recent years, we have seen a growing realization among scientists that the theory of natural causes has a lot of problems. The level of precision and complexity inside a simple cell is staggering, which beggars the imagination regarding how it might have come into being completely by accident.

For example, the amount of information contained in the DNA of a simple cell is so immense that statisticians find it completely impossible for the components of a cell to have been arranged by natural causes and to have spontaneously generated life. One illustration says that believing in natural causes is like believing that a tornado hit a junk yard and built a fully functioning commercial airliner. The probability of that happening is so infinitesimally small as to effectively be zero.

I have a shelf full of books written by biologists, astronomers, physicists, and other scientists who argue that natural causes are an illogical, unreasonable, improbable, irrational, or impossible explanation for the origins of all things. These experts examine thousands of examples of detailed design in our universe and conclude that it couldn't have just happened by any accidental (natural) causes.

On the other hand, the creationists believe that the God of the Bible designed everything, and the ID folks believe that an unnamed source of intelligence designed everything. Both apply the principle that can be illustrated as follows: If I walk through a field and find a rounded pebble, I can assume that the natural forces of wind, erosion, heat, cold, etc. have formed that pebble. However, if I walk through a field and find a fully functioning Rolex watch that is displaying the correct time, I can assume that some intelligent source has designed and built that watch.

When we see a complex piece of machinery or electronic equipment, we instinctively know there was an intelligent designer. An automobile, or a skyscraper, or a computer does not happen by accident. They are designed and built by intelligent beings. In the universe around us, there is exquisitely complex precision everywhere we look. Believing it happened by accident is counterintuitive and illogical.

The ID/creationist folks look at the evidence in nature with those instincts that say that complexity and precision demand an intelligent designer. With the development of more powerful telescopes and more powerful scanning electron microscopes, they can see exquisite design in the smallest to the largest of objects & life forms in the universe. These demand an intelligent designer.

All life requires DNA. The DNA molecule tells the cell what to do. It is like the computer program of the cell. The DNA molecule contains vast amounts of information. It is a string of four proteins several feet long, coiled up inside a DNA molecule. The sequence of those proteins is like the binary or two-digit code of 1s and 0s in a computer code. The string of 1s and 0s forms the information that tells the computer what to do. With a string of 4 proteins, it is like having a 4-digit code. With such a long string plus four digits, the DNA molecule contains an enormous amount of information that tells the cell what to do. The only source of information is an intelligent mind. Think of it like this: the DNA molecule is the computer hardware of the cell, but it needs the input of an intelligent agent to make up the computer software of the cell. Even if it was reasonable to think that the hardware could be assembled naturally, it still needs an intelligent source to program it. Information does not assemble itself by accident. Information demands an intelligent source.

In our environment, we see thousands of examples of meaningful information that was assembled by intelligent beings. Any book or any computer program is a perfect example of detailed information assembled by intelligent beings. We see no (ZERO) examples of meaningful information that was assembled by random accidental chance. You can't dump a box of Scrabble tiles on a table and expect them to naturally spell any meaningful sentence. It is a universal truth that information demands an intelligent source.

Beyond natural vs supernatural causes, we can further subdivide the concept of supernatural creation into two basic categories. We have YEC or Young Earth Creationists who read the Bible quite literally, or maybe I should say superficially, and conclude that everything was created in seven earth days of 24-hour duration each, or in six days of work plus a day of rest. We also have the OEC or Old Earth Creationists who allow that the seven days of Genesis can be interpreted allegorically to be seven longer but finite periods of time, so God created everything in seven stages, or seven creative episodes of a duration suitable to the workday of an eternal God. Both have reasons for their interpretations, reasons that they believe to be irrefutable.

Concepts of origins

Ancient creation myths	Darwinian evolution	Biblical Divine Creation / ID
• Romans	• No God required	• God supernaturally designed and caused
• Greeks	• Natural evolution	• Literal reading
• Egyptians	• Mutations	• 24 hr days - science is wrong
• Mayans	• Survival of the fittest	• 24 hr days – appearance of age
• Incas	• Uncaused / unplanned	• 24 hr days – Gap
• Hopi	• Accidental changes	• Allegorical reading
• Chinese	• Origin of singularity - unknown	• Day age – progressive creation
• Hindu	• Origin of first life – unknown and statistically impossible	• Day age- gradual creation (evolution)
• Japanese		• Punctuated day age – 24 hr days with large gaps between days
• Sumerian		• Intelligent design – no specific god, no specific timeline
• other		• Framework – Moral story unrelated to actual physical origins

By way of full disclosure, I have come to favor the OEC interpretation. Since my youngest days in Sunday School, I have accepted that God is real, and He is the creator. For many years, my only exposure was to a young-earth concept, and I accepted that by faith in spite of not understanding how it made sense. The more I studied the subject, the less satisfied I became with the explanations and interpretations of the YEC approach to the story of creation. Only in the past few years have I "converted" to an old-earth model of creation. Why? Because to believe in a young earth, you need to take many things by blind faith and ignore the contrary evidence you see in the created world we live in. The problem with blind faith is that it can be misled or mistaken. (Witness almost any cult). I don't think the Bible expects us to have blind faith. Peter says to be ready to give a reason for the hope that is in us (1Peter 3:15). If you look in any Bible concordance, references for reasoning are plentiful. So, reason and logic should supplement and strengthen our faith. The whole field of Christian apologetics exists to give us reasons to support our faith.

As I have examined the scientific and the scriptural evidence, I have become convinced that the "days" of creation are longer than 24 hours. Please understand that I do not believe in a long history of the universe because I believe that it all developed accidentally through natural causes (evolution). I also do not believe that God is not capable of creating everything in 144 hours (6 days times 24 hours). I simply believe that the evidence we see in God's creation indicates that God chose to take more than 144 hours to create the universe and everything in it. I guess that is/was His choice.

Some think that believing in days longer than 24 hours is a compromise with evolution and weakens faith. For me, it has been the opposite. The more I see the agreement between true science (not evolution) and Scripture, the more my faith has been strengthened. The more I see that the Scriptures are true and accurate, the more I respect and reverence the Creator God.

Many in the YEC community equate acceptance of long time periods of earth history with acceptance of the theory of evolution by natural causes. The truth is that if you believe in evolution, you must have billions of years of history. However, if you accept billions of years of history in the universe, you can believe in either divine creation by an eternal God or evolution by uncaused natural actions.

In spite of my personal acceptance of an OEC model of creation, I respect and accept Christian brothers and sisters who have a problem with OEC and prefer to embrace a YEC model of creation. If you are one of the folks who has a low aptitude for or a low interest in science, and there are many of you, you may not want to follow the details of an OEC interpretation. It may be easier to accept 24-hour days. For those who equate science with evolution, and do not see a difference between the true data of science and the wild speculations of some popular so-called science, I can easily understand their position regarding 24-hour days, and I can still respect them. I don't accept their position, but I understand it.

Chapter 5:
Creation myths

So, what about the criticism that says the creation story in the Bible is just a myth like hundreds of other creation myths? Why do I think this one is different?

For millennia, men and women of many faiths and belief systems have accepted that there is a Creator God or gods who is (are) responsible for the existence of the natural world. Many religious belief systems, from the most modern to the most ancient, both monotheistic and polytheistic, have some form of creator and some form of creation account. Some very common themes that run through many of them are the ideas of a creator god, original chaos made orderly by that god, and man as the highest order of created beings. Several of the ancient religions & philosophies believe that the cosmos is eternal, but the gods created Earth and all that it contains.

If you accept the old adage that where there is smoke, there must be fire, then these various stories of a creator god are supporting evidence for the existence of a creator god. Somewhere in the distant past, various cultures have had an experience with this creator god – an experience that left an indelible impression. That impression has been handed down through centuries or millennia of their culture, with a fair amount of distortion picked up along the way.

So, what are some of these ancient models known as divine creation? The Bible is certainly not the only creation model that invokes divine supernatural forces. Below is a sample of some creation stories from some of the major ancient religions. There are many more, but these will give you a flavor.

1. The Hindu tradition has various concepts of creation. One refers to a golden egg. One refers to the dismemberment of a cosmic being who is sacrificed to the gods. One claims it was dreamed by their creator god. In short, they do not have a rigid concept of creation beyond the idea of a god being responsible.

2. The Mayans believed that the wind and sky god created the earth as the center of the universe. They believed in a cyclical creation with plants and animals first, then several iterations of humans with progressively higher levels of capability.

3. The Incas believed that either their god Viracocha or Ataguchu created everything. Their narrative changed a bit depending on who was emperor.

4. The Hopi believed that Tawa, the first creator, formed the first world from endless space.

5. The Greeks believed that the universe started with an empty, dark void. Earth was created as a dwelling place for the gods. The gods struggled and fought with each other, creating air, water, plants, animals, and so on. Finally, the gods fashioned man from mud and breathed life into him.

6. The Egyptians believed that Atum created the earth out of a chaos of dark, directionless waters over a long period of time.

7. The Sumerians believed that multiple Gods existed before the earth. They created men as slaves to do their heavy work.

You may notice that some of these beliefs have elements similar to some elements of the Biblical account. Things such as a transcendent pre-existing god, creation out of nothing, original chaos, progression to creation with man as the ultimate & highest life form, and so on are repeated often in these myths. However, none of those myths stands up well to scientific scrutiny.

Also, some people see similarities and conclude that the creation story in the Bible is simply a copy of older creation myths. However, if you examine them carefully, you see that many of the ancient myths come after Genesis in history. If Genesis predates a story, it can't be a copy. Also, if a culture had no communication with the Middle East, there could be no copying. The stories that are older than Genesis lack many of the features of the Genesis account. The gods of these non-Biblical stories are not the Creator God of Genesis.

While these stories tend to add general support for the historical fact of an original creation by a supernatural being, they do not have the scientific accuracy and agreement with the physical evidence that the Biblical creation story has. These myths may have originated as true accounts, but they have been polluted by generations of oral transmission.

Another critical difference is that most of these myths have a god or gods who started with something and reformed it into something else. Often, they have multiple gods who either fought or cooperated on the creation effort, and they used various "tools" to accomplish their purposes. The Creator God of the Bible started with nothing, acted alone, and used only the power of His voice to speak features into existence. The Creator God of the Bible is truly unique. He stands alone as the true creator.

Chapter 6:
Common Interpretations of Gen 1

As you may have gathered, there are a variety of understandings of the account in the first chapter of Genesis. Sincere scholarly men for hundreds or maybe thousands of years have struggled to understand the relationship between what is observed in the cosmos and what is written in Scripture.

For centuries, even before Darwinism, there has been a conflict between what is perceived as scientific evidence for millions or billions of years of earth history and the literal interpretation of the 6 days of Genesis. It is a conflict that is deep-seated in many of us today. On the one hand, we hear what we are taught in church about 6 literal 24-hour days of creation activity about 6000 years ago. On the other hand, we are taught that the universe and indeed planet Earth show evidence of billions of years of history. Often, we accept by faith that God is the creator, but there is still that conflict. Men have struggled to reconcile that conflict.

They have concluded a number of possible interpretations of Genesis. Following are a few of them:

- <u>Creation science</u> – these folks believe that the world was created in 144 hours (6 days times 24 hours per day) about 6000 years ago, and all science that says otherwise derives from a rejection of any god and a belief in natural evolution. They work to rewrite the conclusions of hundreds of years of scientific discovery. They often appeal to the destructive changes left by a universal flood to account for the evidence seen in rocks and fossils today.

- <u>Appearance of age</u> – These folks believe that the world was created in 144 hours about 6000 years ago, but it looks older to scientists because God created it in a mature condition, which appears to be older. They seem to believe that God is either a prankster or a liar. Did He create a tree with tree rings representing years that never existed? Scripture says that God is a God of truth (Num 23:19, 1 Sam 15:29, Ps 31:5, Isaiah 45:19, Isaiah 65:16Heb 6:18).

- <u>Day age</u> – These folks believe that each "day" of creation represents millions of years with God working continuously to form the universe. The days of creation in Genesis are "God days" with a duration suitable to the workday of an eternal God.

- <u>Theistic evolution</u> – These folks believe that God created the inanimate universe and then created the first living cell with the capability to mutate and evolve into the diversity of life that we see today. Then He let natural evolution complete the job of making the diverse life we see today.

- <u>Punctuated 24 hours</u> – These folks believe that each creative act was completed in 24 hours, but God then allowed that bit of creation to mature for millions or billions of years before proceeding to the next creative act, the next day of creation. So, the 6 days were not sequential 24-hour days.

- <u>Gap</u> –These folks believe that Genesis 1:1 describes the original creation, and the rest of the story describes a re-creation of planet Earth after a gap of billions of years at the time of the fall of Lucifer.

- <u>Framework</u> – These folks believe that the 7 days are simply a literary device to give a framework to the creation story. The "days" have no relation to actual time.

- <u>Historical creationism</u> – This view basically teaches that Genesis 1:1 describes the creation of the universe, while the rest of the story describes only the creation of planet Earth as a home for mankind.

There are more, and several of the above include multiple variations & nuances on the main theme. Although I accept parts of some of these, none of them fully satisfy me. I fully believe that there is a creator God who created the universe plus every life form in the universe. When I lay the evidence seen in God's creation alongside the words in His written communication to mankind, I see an agreement. None of the above interpretations seems to fully recognize that agreement.

I should include an important note here. The purpose of the Biblical account is to communicate the who of creation. A belief in the Creator God is vital. The what, the where, and the when of creation are interesting, but they are secondary in importance to a belief in the who of creation. So, if you firmly believe in any of the above interpretations and firmly believe in the Creator God, do not feel compelled to change your belief based on the concept/interpretation I am promoting. However, if you have doubts about any of the traditional interpretations because of the claims of science, please consider the understanding of creation that I am proposing in this book.

Chapter 7:
Misunderstandings

You might be wondering what makes a retired automotive engineer think that the foremost scholars in the fields of science and religion for centuries might be wrong, and that I might have a better interpretation of the story of creation in Scripture? While I recognize that it might be somewhat arrogant of me to think that conventional wisdom is wrong, it would not be the first time in history that the best Bible scholars or the best scientists have been wrong. History has many examples of sincere men reading the Holy Scriptures and making wrong conclusions, and it has many examples of intelligent people making scientific conclusions that have later been proven wrong.

Through the centuries, godly men have interpreted the infallible Word of God in the light of their own biases and perspectives and, in some cases, have just plain gotten it wrong. A classic example of this misinterpretation was the Jewish expectations of a Messiah, which were based on their interpretation of prophecies in the scriptures. The prophecies were true, but their interpretation was so wrong that they rejected and crucified their Messiah when He arrived.

Another classic misinterpretation was the belief that verses like Psalms 102:25 and others say God laid the foundations of the earth, or God fixed the earth in place, or God hung the earth on nothing, so the earth must be fixed in place, the earth must be immoveable, thus planet earth must be the center of the universe with the sun, moon, and stars moving in orbits around planet earth. When scientists proved that the Earth orbits the sun, so it is not the center of the universe, it was very traumatic for the clergy to accept the truth discovered by new evidence. The Catholic church imprisoned Galileo for teaching that the Earth orbits the sun.

 Other misinterpretations of scripture include the Millerites in the mid-1800s who, through their interpretation of scripture, set a date for the Second Coming of our Lord. That date did not materialize. Also, there were southern preachers who misapplied scripture to justify holding Africans in slavery.

So, is a young-earth interpretation another misinterpretation? I ask myself if any of the current religious doctrines about origins are misinterpretations of the true words of the Scriptures. Are there other possible understandings that could be faithful to the truth of scripture but lead to a doctrine that is not antithetical to the observations and measurements made by scientists?

On the other hand, the church is not the sole proprietor of erroneous conclusions. Through the centuries, scientists have made observations of nature and drawn wrong conclusions from their observations. For example, they once believed that since gold and lead (or copper) were both very soft and heavy, there must be a way to convert those cheap metals into gold. Alchemists tried for centuries to find that secret with no success.

Scientists also believed for many years that the development of the Earth took place in a uniform environment of slow, gradual changes. We now know that the history of the Earth is marked by major catastrophes and non-uniformities.

Scientists once believed in the spontaneous generation of life from non-living materials when they saw maggots forming in rotting meat. We now know that flies lay eggs, which hatch into maggots, and in fact, there are no examples of spontaneous generation of life in any form.

Scientists also once believed that the universe is eternal with no beginning. We now know they were wrong. The universe had a beginning. Is Darwinian natural evolution another erroneous conclusion of science?

So, while my interpretations of scripture and science may not be 100% accurate, I have no problem challenging the popular conclusions of the experts of our day.

Chapter 8:
Basic facts of science (physics)

As I noted earlier, many of the books on creation and science are deeply technical and difficult to read and understand. I have read a lot of them, and I have really struggled to stay awake while reading some of them. Sometimes, the best I could do is to take away a simple summary of the key message of the book. This is one of the reasons I set out to write a book that is easier to read and understand.

However, without trying to get too deep into the realm of science, there are a few things that must be understood in order to understand my thesis that Scripture and science tell the same story of origins. At the risk of severely oversimplifying scientific fact, we know that everything in the universe is composed of millions of kinds of molecules. All of those molecules are composed of 94 naturally occurring atoms or elements. Those atoms are built from 17 subatomic particles.

These sub-atomic particles are actually tiny packets of energy. In the early 20th century, Einstein proved to us that all mass consists of energy with his famous formula $E=MC^2$. This was the basis for the atomic bomb and all nuclear energy. With conventional combustion, fuel burns chemically in oxygen, and some molecules are converted to other molecules, but the total number of atoms remains the same. If I put 1 million atoms of oxygen and 2 million atoms of hydrogen into a container and ignite the mix, I end up with 1 million molecules of water (H2O). The end products have the same number of atoms and the same mass as what you started with.

Conversely, atomic energy splits some large atoms into smaller atoms, releasing energy. The number of small atoms you end up with is larger than the number of large atoms you started with. The mass of the end products is less than the mass of the products you started with. The difference is mass that has been converted to energy. If I could put 1 million atoms of uranium in a container and induce a nuclear reaction, I would get 2 million smaller atoms plus a lot of energy. The reverse is also true. If I could concentrate enough energy in the right conditions, I could make an atom from pure energy.

Scripture tells us that God created everything from nothing. More specifically, it says He made that which is seen from that which is not seen (Heb 11:3). He made particles (mass) from energy. That means God supplied the energy to make every atom in the universe. If converting a few grams of mass (atoms) into energy gives us a nuclear weapon capable of destroying a city, imagine the energy/power needed to make all of the trillions of trillions of tons of mass in the universe. Wow!! God's power is inconceivable to our human minds.

If you recall the charts of the periodic table that were posted on the walls of most high school science classrooms, you might recall that everything in the universe, every molecule, is made from the 94 naturally occurring elements (atoms) on that chart. There are also 24 synthetic or man-made elements that do not occur in nature. You might also recall a chart showing that all atoms are made from the 17 subatomic particles with funny names. So, millions of kinds of molecules (materials) are made from 94 different atoms, which are made from 17 subatomic particles.

I am not sure how it fits, but there is a lot of attention being given today to something scientists call "dark matter". They call it dark simply because they don't know what it is. Apparently, it is a particle that does not interact with light, so it is invisible to any of our instruments. However, this particle has mass, so it interacts with gravity. Scientists know it exists because they see the effects of the gravity it produces influencing the motions of heavenly bodies. Imagine the wind that you cannot see directly, but you know it exists because you see it moving tree leaves and flags, and such. In a similar fashion, based on the measured distortions in gravity and the effects of gravity on the motions of planets, stars, and galaxies, scientists estimate that up to 70% of the mass in the universe consists of this dark matter. The problem is that they have never captured a particle of dark matter. They can't put it under a microscope or put it in a test tube or analyze it in any way. It amazes me that people will believe in a particle they cannot directly see, but they refuse to believe in a God that they cannot directly see.

Periodic Table of the Elements

94 naturally occuring elements +
24 synthetic man made elements =
118 total atoms / elements

1 H																	2 He
3 Li	4 Be											5 B	6 G	7 N	8 O	9 F	10 Ne
11 Na	12 Mg											13 Al	14 Si	15 P	16 S	17 Cl	18 Ar
19 K	20 Ca	21 Sc	22 Ti	23 V	24 Cr	25 Mn	26 Fe	27 Co	28 Ni	29 Cu	30 Zn	31 Ga	32 Ge	33 As	34 Se	35 Br	36 Kr
37 Rb	38 Sr	39 Y	40 Zr	41 Nb	42 Mo	43 Tc	44 Ru	45 Rh	46 Pd	47 Ag	48 Cd	49 In	50 Sn	51 Sb	52 Te	53 I	54 Xe
55 Cs	56 Ba	*	72 Hf	73 Ta	74 W	75 Re	76 Os	77 Ir	78 Pt	79 Au	80 Hg	81 Ti	82 Pb	83 Bi	84 Po	85 At	86 Rn
87 Fr	88 Ra	**	104 Rf	105 Db	106 Sg	107 Bh	108 Hs	109 Mt	110 Ds	111 Rg	112 Cn	113 Nh	114 Fl	115 Mc	116 Lv	117 Ts	118 Og

* Lanthanide series	57 La	58 Ce	59 Pr	60 Nd	61 Pm	62 Sm	63 Eu	64 Gd	65 Tb	66 Dy	67 Ho	68 Er	69 Tm	70 Yb	71 Lu
** Actinide series	89 Ac	90 Th	91 Pa	92 U	93 Np	94 Pu	95 Am	96 Cm	97 Bk	98 Cf	99 ES	100 Fm	101 Md	102 No	103 Lr

Subatomic particles			
<u>Quarks</u>	<u>Leptons</u>	<u>Gauge Bosons</u>	
Up	Electron	Gluon	Higgs Boson
Down	Muon	Photon	
Charm	Tau	Z Boson	
Strange	Electron Neutrino	W Boson	
Top	Muon Neutrino		
Bottom	Tau Neutrino		

Everything in the universe is built from these 17 particles

We also know that every particle in the universe is affected by 4 basic forces.

1) The strong nuclear force holds the nuclei of atoms together. Were it not for the strong nuclear force, two positively charged protons would never join together to form the nucleus of an atom.

2) Gravity causes all mass to be attracted to all mass. This one needs very little explanation. The mass of my body is attracted to the mass of planet Earth, so my feet stay on the ground.

3) Electro Magnetic Force (EMF) is what most of us would recognize as "energy". Electricity, magnetism, light (visible light, ultraviolet light, infrared light, microwaves, radio waves, gamma rays, etc.), are all recognized by physicists to be EMF. Also note, EMF is what holds electrons in orbits around atomic nuclei, which makes atoms possible and makes chemical reactions possible to form molecules.

4) The weak nuclear force makes atomic reactions possible. Nuclear fusion, which fuses small atoms into larger atoms, nuclear fission, which splits large atoms into smaller atoms, and

radioactive decay are all possible because of the weak nuclear force.

We also know that while these 4 basic forces are constant across the entire universe, time is not. Time does not pass at the same rate everywhere in the universe. Time passes differently depending on local conditions. So, the relative vantage points of observers make a difference in the rate at which time passes. Scientists call that feature time dilation, and while it sounds like science fiction, it has been proven accurate. More on time dilation later. (meanwhile, Google "time dilation" for an interesting read)

Most of us today assume that time is constant and equal across the universe and that it has always been exactly the same as it is today. However, Einstein's special and general theories of relativity tell us that while the speed of light is constant, the rate at which time passes changes with different conditions. It has been proven true.

Scripture seems to recognize time dilation when it says that with God a thousand years are as a day gone by (Psalms 90:4). In a separate chapter, we will look at how time dilation affects the scriptural story of the timeline of creation.

So, given the reality of time dilation, I have to ask myself what our vantage point, or our local conditions, are compared to the vantage point of an eternal & omnipresent (present everywhere at once) God? Is this the effect the Bible is referring to when it says what looks like a day to God can look like a thousand years to us?

In other words, if God is omnipresent throughout the universe, does the time that looks like a million or a billion years to us look like a day to God? Does a divine "workday" look like millions of years to us earthlings? Sometimes I think that time dilation makes the debate over the timeline of creation look as foolish and petty as the Middle Ages debate over how many angels can dance on the head of a pin.

Chapter 9:
Basic philosophies

As with basic facts of science, there are a few basic philosophies that we should also understand.

Christians for centuries have considered the scriptures, the Bible, to have been inspired by God. In fact, numerous passages in the Bible claim that the collection of scriptures represents the message from God to mankind. God is the essence of truth. He cannot lie, so His inspired words are true. Jesus expanded on this thought when He said that not only are the words of scripture true, but even the tiny punctuation marks are true and will never change (Matt 5:17-18). However, sincere, scholarly, godly men have read the words of scripture and have interpreted their meaning differently or have placed different emphasis on different passages. This is why we have dozens of different denominations within Christianity. Catholics, Lutherans, Anglicans, Baptists, Presbyterians, Methodists, and others all worship Jesus Christ, but they have differences in many of the finer points of theology and practices based on their interpretations or emphasis given to different passages of scripture.

Aristotle said that "it is not the facts that divide men but the interpretation of the facts". If I may paraphrase a bit, it is not the words of Scripture that divide men, but their interpretation of the words. Again, this is why we have dozens of Christian denominations.

So how do we know which interpretation is the correct one? In every case, is one totally right and all others totally wrong, or can there be multiple legitimate meanings/lessons/applications in individual passages of scripture? An old axiom of scripture interpretation says that "in essentials unity, in all else charity," meaning that core beliefs must have agreement, but there are debatable issues that may give different understandings to people with different perspectives, backgrounds, personalities, and levels of Christian maturity. In these areas, we need to treat each other with dignity, respect, and love. We need to disagree agreeably.

The story of creation in the scriptures can have a superficial understanding as well as deeper understandings. What is important and must be agreed by all Christians is that a transcendent, supreme being that we call God exists, and that He created the universe and everything in it. As creator, He has the ultimate authority to rule His creation. I am not sure you can be a genuine Christian without believing that God is our creator, but you can be a good Christian and believe different things about how and when He created every little detail. So, the "who" of creation is critical. On the other hand, there is some room for different interpretations about the what, the where, the when, and the how of the creation story.

This is probably a good place for me to state an important idea once again. I am advocating a specific interpretation of the story of creation in Scripture. I believe it is critical to show people who have been indoctrinated in Darwinian atheistic ideology that the story of creation in scripture is scientifically accurate. By extrapolation, if the story of creation is accurate, the creator God who revealed it must also be real, not mythological.

However, as I noted earlier, if you already have a strong faith and belief in any of several interpretations of the story of creation in scripture, the day age theory, the gap theory, the framework theory, or any of several more (you can look them up to get more details of each) then I am very happy that you believe in the existence of God and His status as creator. I do not want to weaken or challenge your faith. The understanding of the when, the where, and the how of creation is secondary to the belief in the who of creation. The who is critical.

My focus is on building Godly faith in the person who has serious doubts about God's existence or His relevance because of their perception that the story of creation in Scripture is an unscientific myth. The message to those folks is that **<u>Science and Scripture tell the same story of creation</u>**. A creator God does exist, He is a real person, and He is very relevant to your life.

Chapter 10:
Define life

Regardless of how you believe life arose, whether by natural, accidental chance, or by divine will and action, how do you define or recognize life? Oddly enough, scientists do not have a universally accepted definition of life. Most definitions include things such as an ability to absorb and use nutrients, to grow, and to reproduce. Other features of life involve the ability to respond to stimuli, to have a life cycle, to constantly change, and so on. By some definitions, viruses are not living organisms because they require a host cell in order to reproduce. We all think we can recognize a living organism when we see it, but if you look up "definition of life" on the internet, you will find a lot more material than you might imagine for what we normally would consider to be a simple question with an obvious answer.

At least as far back as the ancient Greek philosophers, scholars have debated the definition of life. What makes an organism alive? What is the "magic" that makes a group of cells to be alive. If we look at a lab rat that is running around, we say it is alive. If that lab rat dies, the dead body has the same cells as it had a moment before it died. Why is that group of cells alive one moment and dead the next? It seems that life must be more than just a collection of, or a complex choreography of, chemical reactions.

Since the mid-20th century, there have been a lot of studies of the stories told by persons who have had near-death experiences (NDE) or out-of-body experiences (OBE). Researchers in several countries have interviewed over a thousand people who have been clinically dead (no pulse, no respiration, no brain wave activity) and later revived, often autonomously. These people report accurately on things that happened while they were physically dead. These reports are not limited to things that happened in the room where their dead body was located, but also include things that happened in other rooms and even outside of the building where their body was located. Apparently, their consciousness was able to move about, see and hear things, think, feel, and remember things, totally apart from their physical body and brain.

Again, if you search the internet for material on NDEs or OBEs, you will find much more information than what I am presenting here. I mention the issue only to emphasize that the definition of human life involves much more than DNA, chemistry, & biological functions. There seems to be an ethereal element that science recognizes but can't define. We humans have a consciousness that is separate from our physical bodies. Our consciousness continues to exist and function after our physical body is dead. Life, especially human life, is so much more than a complex choreography of chemical reactions.

Life in any form is a mystery to us. We can dissect an animal and learn all about the circulatory system and the nervous system and the bones and the muscles, and everything else. We can analyze the chemicals in each part of the animal body, and we can identify individual animals by their unique DNA. We can understand the behavior and psychology of an animal. We can tell when an animal is alive or dead, and we can certainly make a living animal dead. We can even bring animals back from the brink of death. However, we cannot identify life itself. We cannot put "life" under a microscope and examine it. We can't hold it in our hands, see it, taste it, etc. We also have never been able to take a set of inert, lifeless chemicals and make them come alive. It takes God to do that.

While science has difficulty defining life in general and human life in particular, the Bible simply says that God created each form of life. In the case of humans, the Bible says that God breathed into them the "breath of life" and He created man "in the image of God" (Genesis 1:26). The description of the "image of God" is only applied to humans. This raises two questions. First, what is this breath of life? Second, what does it mean to be created in the image of God?

I believe you can visualize the "image of God" by comparing His triune divine being (Father, Son, and Holy Ghost) to human triune beings (Body, Mind, and Spirit). Scripture says we have an eternal soul, and science says we have a consciousness beyond and apart from our physical body. Again, **Scripture and science tell the same story of origins (27)**.

The existence of a soul (the image of God) seems to be the thing that makes humans unique among the animals. While we have a physical body similar to that of many animals, we are much more than a mere animal. We have the ability to think abstractly, we have the ability to communicate in complex language, and we also have the ability to communicate with and worship a creator God. In fact, when scientists are studying ancient artifacts from ancient cultures, one of the distinguishing factors that identifies a culture as truly human Homo Sapiens vs prehuman or what science calls hominin creatures is any evidence of worshiping any kind of supernatural god.

Chapter 11:
First Life

The scientific concept of the Big Bang addresses the science behind the creation of all the inanimate materials and forces in the universe. The concept of progressive changes or evolution (natural or supernatural) addresses the development of all the diversity of life forms on planet Earth. However, neither the Big Bang nor the evolution theory addresses the appearance of the first life. How does an assembled collection of inanimate, non-living materials suddenly become alive? There is a huge jump from non-living to living.

There are really four questions regarding the first life to form.

- First, how were the materials necessary for life (the proteins, the sugars, the lipids, the amino acids, the aldehydes, and many more) formed from the base elemental materials available in the environmental conditions of the early Earth?

- Second, how did those materials necessary for life become arranged in the precise structure required for a living cell to function?

- Third, what energy made those assembled materials start to function as a living cell?

- Where did the DNA information necessary to manage and regulate the functions in that first cell come from?

Science has no clear answer to any of those questions. They only have speculations.

A somewhat poor analogy might be one of my diesel engines.

- How do we get a cylinder block and a crank and pistons and valves, and so on, from a pile of iron ore and aluminum ore and copper ore, and so on? We can make all of the precise pieces of the engine, but it takes intelligent actions and skills. Those parts do not naturally make themselves from the raw materials.

- Next, how do we assemble those components into an engine? We can install the components in their correct places and in their correct orientations. We can put fuel and lube oil into that engine. Again, that takes intelligence and skill to do so. However, that engine is not running. It is just a nice, precise set of inanimate parts.

- It is not running until we apply some electricity (energy) to the starter motor and make it all start to function as a fully functioning running engine. In the same way, you can assemble all of the chemical pieces of a human or animal body or even an amoeba, but it is not "alive" until it is energized by a force we still do not understand.

- It is also not running until we have a computer programmed to make the functions occur at the correct time and correct strength. In the engine, that is an ECU (engine control unit). In a living cell, it is DNA.

- The Big Bang Theory does not deal with creation of life; it deals only with inanimate materials and forces

Creation / formation of life = A huge jump

- Evolution does not deal with creation of life; it only deals with diversification of species after life exists

Scientists who subscribe to a Darwinian philosophy believe that all life forms evolved from a common source, which is described as a single-celled organism. Let's assume for the moment that it is accurate. Where did that first living cell come from?

The best answer those scientists can come up with is that the first living cell spontaneously (accidentally) developed from a primordial soup that provided all of the right molecules in all of the right proportions and somehow miraculously arranged them in the right structure and provided the spark of energy that made it become alive. They believe that natural chemical reactions in the early Earth's atmosphere were responsible for generating the building blocks required for the first living cell. Those building blocks include a big array of organic chemicals. Any of dozens of different proteins, amino acids, lipids, sugars, fatty acids, amines, aldehydes, and more are required in order to assemble a single living cell. The first question that needs to be answered is: could those chemicals have formed through natural chemical reactions in the ancient Earth's atmosphere and oceans?

Darwinists will often point to an experiment by Stanley Miller in 1953, where he made some amino acids from a mix of chemicals and energy that he supposed represented the ancient primordial ambient conditions. Since then, his mix of materials has been shown not to represent any ancient conditions. Besides that, his experiment was crafted and managed by an intelligent guide. It was hardly random or natural. Also, a few amino acids are a long way from making proteins and DNA molecules. Even so, his work is still included in textbooks as representing the creation of life in a test tube. Contrary to how it is sometimes presented, Stanley Miller did not create life in a test tube. In fact, no one has ever created life in a test tube.

Since Miller's experiment, dozens or maybe hundreds of scientists have shown that the chemicals necessary for life can be formed in a test tube under conditions that they suppose might represent early primordial conditions on planet Earth. They will use ammonia, methane, various carbon compounds, and other simple chemicals, then pass them through a source of energy such as an electrical spark, ultraviolet light, or heat, or shock waves, or other energy sources. These experiments have produced many (not all) of the complex organic chemicals needed to assemble a simple cell.

However, there are several problems with their concept:

- There is no generally accepted consensus among scientists as to what the early Earth's primordial conditions might have been, nor for how long those conditions existed. No one knows how concentrated or diluted the base simple chemicals may have been.

- Scientists generally use highly concentrated solutions in their experiments because the more concentrated the base simple chemicals are, the more likely it is that they will form the more complex chemicals the experimenter is looking for. If those chemicals were heavily diluted in the early Earth, and they most likely were heavily diluted, it would have taken much longer for them to react, and those reactions would have produced much less of the complex material if they produced any at all.

- Many of those complex chemicals are unstable in the presence of oxygen or other chemicals, so if the early Earth atmosphere had very much oxygen or other destructive chemicals, then those complex hydrocarbon chemicals that were produced would have been destroyed before they could have been assembled into a cell.

- You need <u>all</u> of the long list of chemicals to make a living cell. However, different chemicals are formed under different conditions. The conditions that make one chemical will destroy another, so it is impossible to have them all formed from the same conditions in the same primordial soup.

So, when you hear some news report or read in a textbook that a scientist has created some chemical necessary for life through some chemical process in some chemistry lab, please be aware that there are a lot of unknown factors, any of which could likely invalidate that scientist's base assumptions about the early Earth conditions. If early Earth conditions were what that scientist assumes, then yes, it is a valid claim. If early Earth conditions were not what was assumed, then the claim is invalid.

For the sake of argument, let's assume for the moment that all of the hundreds of unique chemical compounds necessary to build a simple cell could have been manufactured by natural means in the early Earth atmosphere and oceans. I doubt that, but for the sake of argument, let's assume for the moment that it is true. The next question that must be answered is: How did those chemicals become assembled in the right structure to form an original simple cell creature?

Once upon a time, spontaneous generation of life might have sounded plausible. In the microscopes of yesteryear, a single-cell creature looked like a blob of protoplasm with skin around it. However, thanks to the development of very powerful scanning electron microscopes and other techniques, we now know that the number of unique molecules needed, plus the precise structure needed among those molecules, is incredibly complex. Not only that, but we know that there is a minimum amount of that complexity that is necessary to support even the simplest life. In other words, it is impossible to have half a cell and call it alive. You cannot be "half alive."

When molecular biologists examine simple single-cell organisms under powerful modern instruments, they see some very interesting structures and systems. At a molecular level, these cells have features analogous to a modern factory. They have structures & systems to regulate the materials incoming. They have structures and systems to dispose of waste products. They have structures and systems to move materials around inside the cell. They have DNA molecules to act as a computer controlling all of the activities in the cell. They have systems to maintain and repair the cell. They have systems to reproduce and deliver new cells. They even have motors and "propellers" to move themselves around in their environment. In short, they have an amazing molecular structure, and all of those structures must be in place for the cell to function.

By way of an illustration, let me say that I spent most of my career engineering diesel engines. (Oh no, not another diesel engine analogy) For one of my engines to function, it must have all of the components (pistons, rods, crank, valves, etc) completely and precisely formed and arranged in the correct locations. I can't make a cylinder block one day and have it function, then add a piston the next day and make it function better, then add a crankshaft the next day and make it function even better, and so on. All of the necessary pieces must be precisely built and properly assembled before the engine will run. I also cannot put a piston upside down or a camshaft backwards and have it function. The same is true of living cells. They must have all of the right molecules in all of the precisely correct places in order to support the first life.

Not only do all of the component pieces of my diesel engine need to be properly assembled for it to function, but I also need to have an engine controller properly programmed to make all of those pieces work together. That controller is like the DNA in a cell. The DNA tells the cell how to function. Like my engine controller, the DNA requires vast amounts of information, and information can only come from a source of intelligence.

Scientists and mathematicians have studied the probability of all the molecules of a simple cell being collected and arranged in the exact necessary structure through natural (accidental) forces. Imagine having a million diverse Lego blocks in a box, and you throw them on a table. What is the probability that natural forces will arrange them in the form of a modern city? Different folks use different assumptions to calculate the probability of natural forces arranging the chemicals of life, possibly existing in a primordial soup, into the structure of a simple cell. Each of them comes up with odds that are astronomically against the spontaneous or accidental generation of the first living cell. In addition, there has never been an observed case of spontaneous generation of life. It never happens. A first life couldn't have "just happened."

In the face of these astronomical odds, the Darwinists resort to the argument that billions of years give a lot of chances for the structure to spontaneously assemble, and it only needs to happen once. What they ignore is that geological evidence shows that the first life arose in a very short time frame. It is well documented that the early conditions on planet Earth were extremely hot. It was too hot for any life to exist, even extremophiles. As the planet cooled, it reached a point where life could exist. If we compare that point on the timeline of planet Earth to the point where we start to see fossils of microscopic creatures, we find that there is a fairly short time available for life to have developed naturally from inanimate materials. From the time when life could have existed until the time when it did exist is a short interval. So, the billions of years that the Darwinists need in order to support their spontaneous generation theory simply were not available.

Possibly even more amazing than the physical structure of living cells is the difference between an inanimate collection of molecules and a living cell. The ethereal element of life is the stuff that makes a batch of cells, or even a single cell creature, with some amazing chemistry and structure, become alive. So, even if the statistically impossible arrangement of cells were to accidentally form, it still would not be alive. "Life" is much more than a complex choreography of chemical elements. It needs the energy (dare I say "spirit") or the stuff that is impossible to measure to make it become alive, to grow, and to reproduce more of its own kind. Scientists have no concept of what that energy/spirit might be. The author of life needs to empower life.

Science has struggled to figure out how life began. The difference between living and non-living things involves vast amounts of information. Science knows that DNA molecules are a string of four proteins that make up coded information (like a computer code) that controls the function, the maintenance, the growth, and the reproduction of the living cell, the most basic element of living things. The plain fact is that every living cell in the universe contains DNA with vast amounts of information that controls its structure and its chemical reactions. Life requires information to exist, and information requires a source of intelligence. Meaningful information does not assemble itself by accident.

Science has no explanation for where the original information (the original computer program) for the original first cell came from. Once there is life, scientists have a lot of theories (not proofs) about how life might have diversified through DNA mutations (natural or supernatural?), but they have no theory, only wild speculations, about how the first cell with a DNA "computer" loaded with information came into existence. Note that you cannot have life without information, and you cannot have information without a source of intelligence.

Information can only be created by intelligence. The second law of thermodynamics says that natural systems progress toward less organization, less information, not more information. We have thousands of examples of meaningful information being created by intelligent sources (books, music, codes, structures, etc.), but we have zero examples of meaningful information being created by totally random natural actions. The only evidence we have says it takes intelligence to create meaningful information. So, that first living cell with a DNA "computer" full of information had to be formed by an external source, an intelligent designer.

Perhaps the classic illustration of intelligent design says that if I walk through a field and find a stone, I can assume that the natural forces of wind, sun, rain, and erosion have shaped that stone. However, if I walk through a field and find a functioning Rolex watch that is showing the correct time, I have to assume that some intelligent source designed, built, and programmed that watch. When we study living cells through a scanning electron microscope, we see a level of complexity that makes a Rolex watch look like a child's plaything. This level of complexity demands an intelligent source to design and build it.

Scripture says that God is the source of life, so He is the source of the information to make the first living cell. Science says they don't know where the information came from. Some have appealed to random chance to get the millions of molecules in the first living cell to become arranged in just the right structure to make a living cell. Statisticians have tried to calculate the odds of such a random event happening. They come up with different numbers, but all of them show an infinitesimally small chance of that happening by accident. Therefore, the only remaining option is an intelligent designer such as the God of creation.

The Darwinists ask me to believe in the spontaneous generation of the first life from inanimate materials in the face of astronomical odds against it? Give me a break! Talk about blind faith.

Chapter 12:
A Matter of Generations

One of the pieces of evidence that Darwinists point to as proof that once life exists, natural evolution is a reasonable explanation for the diversity of life is the fact that disease germs, either viruses or bacteria, can naturally develop DNA mutations that make them resistant to certain medicines. However, when their evidence is examined more closely, the argument falls apart.

Studies on viruses and bacteria (Pneumonia, malaria, AIDs, etc.) have found that these natural mutations do happen, but they are very rare. To produce a beneficial mutation requires very large populations (tens of millions) and many generations (thousands). Since these disease germs reproduce rapidly with very short life cycles (hours), you get those large populations and many generations in a matter of days or weeks.

Also, since only one or two mutations to their DNA are required to develop resistance to a medicine, that resistance can develop fairly quickly. However, even after the mutations, a malaria germ is still a malaria germ and a pneumonia germ is still a pneumonia germ, and so on. Those mutations have never produced a new creature, only a new "breed" or a new strain of the original creature.

Also, even though the mutated germ is resistant to a specific antibiotic, it is generally less robust toward other environments.

If we apply the data learned from these simple creatures to a somewhat more complex creature like a fruit fly, we get different results. There is a longer but still relatively short life cycle (maybe weeks). There is slower, but still fairly rapid population growth. Even so, beneficial natural mutations have not appeared after more than 100 years (several thousand generations) of fruit fly studies.

In 1908, a researcher named Thomas Hunt Morgan started to conduct genetic experiments with fruit flies. He chose fruit flies because with their short life cycle, he could get a lot of generations in a reasonable time. So, geneticists have been studying fruit flies since long before DNA was discovered and understood. They have seen a lot of variation built into the fruit fly DNA. They have seen long wings, short wings, straight wings, curly wings, long legs, short legs, spots, stripes, and more, but all were still fruit flies. While they have never seen a natural DNA mutation, they have artificially forced mutations with radiation. These have given some very weird, grotesque features, none of which could be said to be beneficial to the survival of the fruit fly. None of which changed the fruit fly into a new creature.

Now, if we apply the fruit fly experience to the evolution of an even more complex creature, we could look at the evolution of a chimp into homo sapiens. After all, we are told that the two species share over 90% common DNA. In this case, we not only have a much longer life cycle (years) and a much smaller population growth, but we also require thousands of mutations to get 10% of the DNA to evolve from chimp DNA to human DNA. If you crank through the math, you find that there are not nearly enough years since the first chimp appeared in the fossil record to produce this kind of change by natural mutations. In fact, there are not enough years since the beginning of the Big Bang. You simply do not have enough time to generate the populations and numbers of generations needed. As unreal as this idea is, it doesn't even consider the millions of mutations and trillions of years required to get from a single cell amoeba to a chimp, which makes the problem of single cell amoeba to human evolution multiple times less likely to have developed by natural means.

The Darwinists make a fairly basic mistake when they extrapolate microevolution into macroevolution. What is often called microevolution is very common. It is how we get various breeds of animals. By selective breeding or natural crossbreeding, we can get many breeds of dogs, cats, chickens, cows, and so on. However, none of them become a new family of creatures or a new genus capable of reproducing more of their own kind. When we selectively breed dogs, we can get big ones and small ones, we get long hair and short hair, we get different colors and a lot of variations, but they are all dogs. Macro evolution would be cross-breeding a cat and a dog to get a totally new class of animal. It might also be zapping a dog's DNA to make it into a totally new class of creature. Macro evolution never happens, but this is the erroneous foundation for Darwinian evolution.

Let's face it, folks. Diversity of life by natural mutations is a defunct theory. It takes an intelligent designer and builder, a supreme being, to make the animal kingdom what we see today.

Chapter 13:
What is a "day" (YEC)?

Possibly the biggest obstacle most people have to accepting the biblical story of creation as truth rather than myth is the very short timeline suggested by the 7-day wording in Genesis, compared to the observed universe, which seems to show a much longer history. In any discussion of creation, the length of the creation "day" tends to be the 500-pound gorilla in the room.

A casual reading of Genesis suggests that the universe and all life in it were created in 6 normal 24-hour earth days, followed by a 24-hour day of rest. The YEC folks take that very literally, believing it means 6 current length days of 24 hours (one rotation of the axis of planet earth) or 144 hours. They have a number of fairly convincing-sounding arguments from scripture to back up their position. They examine all scientific evidence based on their conviction that God created everything in a very short period of time fairly recently. Then they conclude that God created everything in a very short period of time fairly recently. Dare I say circular reasoning?

- One line of reasoning says that when the word for "day" in scripture is paired with an ordinal numbering (first, second, third, etc.), it always means a 24-hour earth day. One author that I read claims that the word for day paired with a number is used over 200 times in the Bible, and every time it clearly means a 24-hour day. However, he did not give 200 references so that his claim could be verified. Also, there are numerous uses of the word in scripture where it clearly means a finite by undefined longer period of time. What is the day of the Lord and so on. Also, there are applications in ancient secular Hebrew writings of that era where the word for day is paired with an ordinal numbering, and it does not mean a 24-hour day. In Acts 7:22, the Bible tells us that Moses was learned in all the wisdom of the Egyptians and was mighty in words. Considering that Moses was highly educated in the writings of his day and an excellent communicator, he might very well have used an alternate meaning of the word for day.

- Another line of thought says that the phrase "there was evening and there was morning the first (thru sixth) day can only mean a 24-hour day. However, it also seems that the term evening can mean the twilight or fading of one age of creation, and the word morning can mean the dawn or beginning of the next age of creation. Once again, the YEC interpretation is a valid one, but not necessarily an exclusive one.

- Another line of reasoning says that since plants were created on day 3, the sun was created on day 4, and insects created on day 5, the days must have been short because with no sun, the plants would have quickly died, and with no insects to pollinate them, they could not have reproduced. (I will say more about this later).

- Another line of reasoning says that since God called the creation done on each day good, it could not have included death because God is not the author of death. So, physical death only entered the world when Adam sinned (more on that later too). So, the days must have been short, or the food chain would not have been possible. Note that if God created life with a cycle that included birth, growth, maturity, and death, He could certainly call it good. I suspect calling it good had more to do with the absence of sin. With no sin, it would be good in the eyes of God. It would be functioning according to His design & His wishes.

So, how do the YEC folks explain the apparent age of the earth as observed and measured by scientists?

- One theory believes that all of the geological evidence for a much older Earth is a result of catastrophic changes made at the time of the great flood of Noah about 5000 years ago. While I recognize that a global flood would have caused a lot of damage and left a lot of evidence, I have trouble seeing "all" of the geological evidence being a result of the flood of Noah. This explanation also ignores astronomical and other evidence for an old earth/universe, which would not have been affected by a flood.

- Another theory says that everything looks old to scientists because God created it in a mature state, which made it look old. This makes God either a prankster or a liar, a position which I categorically reject. Did God create a mature tree or millions of mature trees with growth rings for years that did not exist? Did God create mature glaciers with annual snowfall layers for years that did not exist? He certainly could have done that, but would it have been consistent with His character?

- Another theory says that all of the measured evidence observed by scientists is just plain wrong and possibly diabolical. These folks believe that scientists interpret their observations to mean eons of time only because those scientists believe in naturalistic evolution, which requires long periods of time. These folks are trying to rewrite many of the interpretations of scientific observations and measurements discovered in the past several centuries to make them agree with their hypothesis. They claim that things like the amount of sediment on the sea floor, the amount of salt in ocean water, the rate of decay in the earth's magnetic field, the rate at which the moon's orbit is receding away from earth, and more all indicate a young earth. Some of their new interpretations of measured data tend to somewhat stretch the limits of credibility. Their interpretations are often just as speculative as the theories they criticize, and often their calculations still indicate a longer time frame than the 6000 years they allow.

- When I read the writings of YEC advocates, I get the sense that they indulge in the same kind of circular reasoning that they criticize in the evolutionists. They believe that the only true literal meaning of the word "day" in Genesis is a 24-hour sunrise-to-sunrise day, so everything else that they read in scripture is interpreted to support their belief. So, they believe that a selected passage proves a 24-hour day because they believe in a 24-hour day.

Also, some of the major YEC advocates seem to have a holier-than-thou attitude. It is somewhat offensive. They criticize the OEC advocates by saying that the only reason they accept an old earth is because they wish to compromise with the Darwinian theory of natural evolution. Not true. The concept of creation days longer than 24 hours goes back to fourth-century church fathers, centuries before Darwin. Early scholars asked how the first three days could be 24 hours when the sun and moon, which define a 24-hour day, were not created until day four. They proposed an allegorical reading of the word "day". However, the Catholic church decided that the days could only be 24-hour days, so all other discussion was halted. Note that the Catholic church also once dogmatically believed that the sun orbits the Earth.

Some YEC advocates also claim that if you do not agree with their interpretation of the 6 days of creation about 6000 years ago, you cannot be a true Christian. Their dogmatism is a substantial barrier to many who are seeking God but have doubts about creation in 144 hours, about 6000 years ago.

I have read a book that claims to be a comprehensive defense of a young-earth interpretation and a critique of an old-earth interpretation. Quite honestly, in general, most of the arguments seemed to me to be quite convoluted, contrived, and shallow. I also note that YEC advocates seem to see no difference between the inerrancy of the Word of God and the inerrancy of their interpretation of the Word of God. At times, they seem more devoted to their interpretation of Scripture than what they are to the Scripture itself.

Possibly one of my biggest surprises has been the lack of a coup de gras by the YEC folks. I am not a Hebrew language expert, but it seems to me that if Moses had had an alternate Hebrew word available to mean an era, or an age, or an eon, he would have used that word if he had meant to say an era or age or eon. If I knew that such a word existed, and Moses did not use it, it would be an extremely strong argument for understanding the day to be 24 hours.

I read one author who suggested that the Hebrew word "olam" could have been used to signify a longer period of time if that is what God had intended. However, a quick study of that word finds that its meaning is more related to the idea of eternity or forever than what it is related to a finite but undefined long period of time. You cannot have a first eternity and a second eternity and so on.

So, I am still looking for a word that could have been used instead of "yom" to signify an age or era, so we still have the uncertainty. With all of the Hebrew language experts who support YEC, I have not yet read anything by any of them to suggest that such a word existed. Therefore, the definition of the creation "day" has to remain open. The true meaning is dependent on the context.

Chapter 14:
What is a "day" (OEC)?

As you may have noticed, the more I studied the subject of creation, the more I had problems with some of the arguments in support of a literal geosolar 24-hour day of creation. While I respect the YEC folks, most of their arguments regarding the length of a Genesis creation day seem shallow and unconvincing to me. A lot of it involves a sort of circular reasoning. In other words, they believe this or that scripture passage supports creation in 6 days of 24 hours because they believe the days of creation are 24 hours.

On the other hand, the OEC folks have some convincing arguments for a much older universe and planet Earth. Following are a few of those:

- We now know from measured data that the universe is expanding. If you chart the paths of galaxies today and run that video in reverse for 13.8 billion years, everything converges back into a singularity the size of a single atom, and you arrive at a beginning about 13.8 billion years ago. This expansion is the basis for the Big Bang theory. Note that the term "Big Bang" was coined by an atheist who rejected the idea of a beginning because a beginning requires a cause, and evolution/atheism requires uncaused changes. The term was intended to ridicule the concept of a beginning, but the Big Bang terminology stuck.

- We also know from measured data that the light from the most distant stars in the universe started traveling toward us about 13 billion years ago. We see a lot of stars younger and nearer than that, but none older and farther away.

- On day 4 in the scriptural account, God set the stars in place to determine times and seasons (Genesis 1:14). So, if God set the stars in place to be a calendar for mankind, and if that stellar calendar tells us a beginning happened 13.8 billion years ago, why do we not believe it?

- Like the English word "day", the Hebrew word for "day" (Yom) can have multiple meanings. One is certainly a 24-hour day. One is the daylight hours. Another is the length of a workday (OBTW… what is the length of a workday for an eternal God for whom a thousand years are as a day gone by?). The other is more like what we today would call an era, a finite but undefined length of time. Even in modern English, we use the word day multiple ways. If I say that in "Ben Franklin's day, gentlemen wore powdered wigs," you do not understand the word to mean 24 hours. When scripture talks about the "day of the Lord," it is clearly not referring to a 24-hour day. So, it is not imperative to understand the day to be 24 hours. Note too that Biblical Hebrew had no other term to specifically say an era or age, so Moses had no other word choice available to signify an era or a "day" longer than 24 hours. So, we have to look for other clues to know the true meaning of the word in this application. Also, note that while the YEC folks claim their understanding of the word "day" is a literal reading of scripture and they criticize the OEC understanding as an allegorical reading. The fact that the word can have four meanings means that any of the four understandings is a literal reading of scripture.

- Time dilation, which we will discuss in detail later, makes the subject of time pretty irrelevant. In brief, time dilation is a proven fact that says time does not pass at the same rate everywhere in the universe. If (since) scripture tells us that with God a day is as a thousand years and if (since) God is eternal and omnipresent (present everywhere), then His perception of time and our perception of time can be (almost certainly are) two totally different things. What looks like a day to God can easily look like a much longer period of time to us. An eternal God who is omnipresent (present everywhere at once) can call any length of time a day. What looks to us like it must have required an extremely long time to build is just a day's work for an eternal, all-powerful, omnipresent God.

- In Genesis, the first six days of creation end with a repeat of the statement "there was evening and there was morning the "X"th day" (1st day, 2nd day, 3rd day, etc.) …. (Genesis 1:5,8,13,19,23,31). This seems to be a statement declaring that day "X" has ended. That one day is completed, and the next day is beginning. This statement is not included for day seven, the day God rested from His creative works. Was the omission an oversight? I doubt it. I expect it is significant. Today, God is still resting from His works of creation. He is not creating any new materials (particles, elements, atoms, etc), any new forces (electricity, magnetism, gravity, etc), or any new life forms, so it appears that day seven has not ended. We are still in day 7 and have been since Adam & Eve were created several thousand years ago. If day 7 is the era of human history, then we are still in day seven. So, I ask myself, if day seven is several thousand years long, how long were each of the first six days?

- As early as the 4th century, church fathers questioned how days one through three could be sunrise to sunrise days or 24-hour days when the sun had not been made to separate day from night until day four. The sequencing seems to eliminate the possibility of the days being normal-length Earth days. Again, did God make a mistake in the narrative? I doubt it.

- While it doesn't prove millions of years of Earth history, ice cores taken in the deep glaciers of Greenland and Antarctica show annual snowfall layers dating back over 100,000 years. Much longer than YEC advocates allow for the age of the Earth. Did God create ice layers for years that did not exist? That does not seem to mesh with the concept of a God of truth.

- While the YEC folks completely dismiss the science of radiometric dating. It has been used for decades and has been repeatedly refined and calibrated. Measuring the radioactive decay of trace elements in rocks and comparing it to the known half-life of those elements has given ages for rocks on planet Earth (and the moon) in the range of a few billion years. Even if those calculations are off by 99.9%, the age of the Earth is still millions of years old, well over the 6000 years that YEC folks allow. Did God create rocks with radioactive decay for years that did not exist? Again, that does not seem to be consistent with the character of a God of truth.

- The YEC folks reject the idea of using the observed facts from physics, astronomy, and other disciplines to clarify the meaning of passages regarding creation. However, for decades or maybe centuries, Biblical archeologists have used their observations from archeological digs to clarify the meanings of Biblical passages. Why do they accept the findings of one science and reject the findings of others? It seems completely acceptable to me to use observations of God's world to clarify our understanding of God's Word.

These are a few of my reasons for believing in an old earth with a creation timeline longer than seven current earth days of 24 hours each.

Note that beginning in Chapter Two of Genesis, the story shifts from creation to the history of mankind. The OEC folks (like myself) do not necessarily dispute the idea of six to ten thousand years of human history after creation was completed, after Adam & Eve. The oldest scientific estimate I have heard for true human (Homo Sapiens) existence is about 50,000 years, but that seems to be an outlier. A more typical scientific date for the existence of true humans is in the six to ten thousand-year range. What OEC folks consider old is the first chapter of Genesis, the creation itself, from the beginning up to and including Adam.

The OEC folks firmly believe that there is a Creator God who supernaturally created everything, and they firmly believe that He did it in a sequence of 6 "days" from the beginning up to and including the creation of the first humans. They simply believe that the evidence we see in God's creation indicates that those 6 "days" are something longer than 24 hours each, and the account in scripture allows for that interpretation.

Note that the YEC folks seem to equate a belief in longer days or ages with a belief in naturalistic evolution. The truth is that while naturalistic evolution requires long ages of time to even sound reasonable, long ages of time do not automatically prove evolution to be a true concept. Unlike natural evolution, supernatural divine creation can happen in either short days or long ages of time.

If you are convinced that God created everything in 6 days of 24-hour duration, I will not question your belief in divine creation, nor your devotion to the creator God, nor your acceptance of the Bible as God's word to mankind. On the other hand, I insist that you not question my belief in divine creation, nor my devotion to the creator God, nor my acceptance of the Bible as God's word to mankind if I am convinced that the days of creation are longer than 24 hours.

Please let me be perfectly clear. I do not believe in an old earth because I accept the Darwinian theory of natural evolution as a reasonable explanation for the origins of life and the diversity of life. There is no compromise here. I simply conclude that the evidence indicates God chose to take more than 144 hours to create the universe. The creation timeline is clearly at the whim of the creator.

By the way, I also do not believe in an old earth because I believe God is not capable of making everything in six days of 24 hours. Could he do that? Yes, he could. He could do it in six days of 24 seconds if He chose to do it like that. The real question is, did He choose to do it in that time frame, and is that what He means by the six days narrative? The evidence in the universe he created seems to say He chose a much longer time frame.

How eternal and timeless is your god?

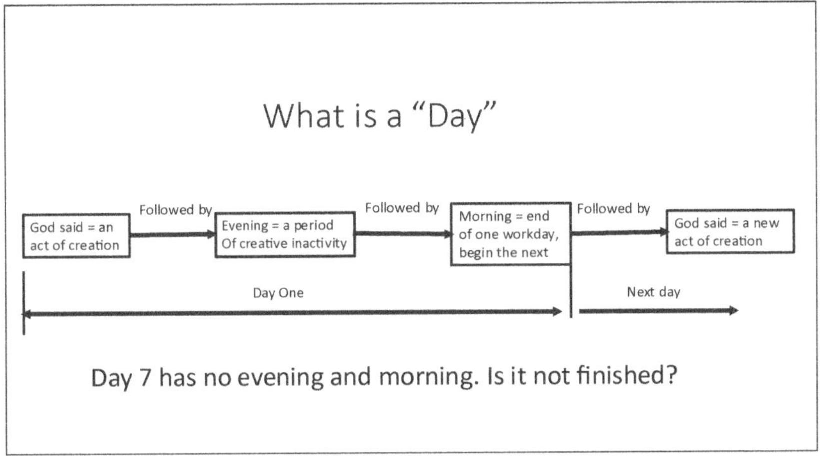

Chapter 15:
Time dilation

OK, I have mentioned time dilation several times. Now it is probably time for me to give a more in-depth explanation.

Einstein's theories of relativity first predicted that time is affected by the local conditions where the time is being measured. The rate at which time passes is different for observers in different conditions, most notably conditions of velocity and gravity.

Since Einstein, science has proven that time is affected by the relative velocity of the observers. The Hafele-Keating experiment in 1970 placed atomic clocks in a stationary lab (actually moving through space at the speed of rotation of the surface of earth) and put other identical atomic clocks on a series of commercial jet airliners traveling around the globe east to west (slower than the stationary lab) and yet another set on a series of airliners flying west to east (faster than the lab). When the traveling clocks were brought back to the lab, they displayed different times than the clocks that had been stationary in the lab. The velocity of the traveling clocks had changed the rate at which time passed for those clocks.

When men started traveling in space, scientists also confirmed that the rate at which time passes is affected by gravity. One theory says that if I could stand on the edge of a black hole with gravity so intense that even light cannot escape (that is why it is black), time would stand still due to the intense gravity.

A perfect example of the fact that time is affected by velocity and gravity is the GPS device that we all carry around in our cell phones. We all use GPS without thinking about how it works. It works when dozens of satellites parked in the zero gravity of space, in geosynchronous orbits (traveling through space faster than anything on the surface of the planet), use very precise atomic clocks to each continuously send out a signal telling the satellite's location and the time the signal was sent.

Your GPS receiver on Earth also has a very precise atomic clock. It checks the time the signal was received and calculates how long it took the signal to travel from the satellite to your GPS device. Knowing the speed of the signal and the time it took to travel between the two devices, it calculates the distance between the satellite and your device. Think of a car traveling 70 mph for two hours travels 140 miles, so a signal traveling at X miles per second for Y seconds travels X times Y miles. With 3 or more of these distances, your device triangulates your position on the Earth.

One problem the developers of the GPS system had to overcome was the fact that for a satellite traveling at high speeds in the low gravity of an orbit in outer space, time passes slightly differently than it does on the face of the Earth, where there is 1 G of gravity. The difference is only about 7 microseconds (millionths of a second) per day, but with accuracy depending on extremely precise atomic clocks that measure time in nanoseconds (billionths of a second), that difference is crucial.

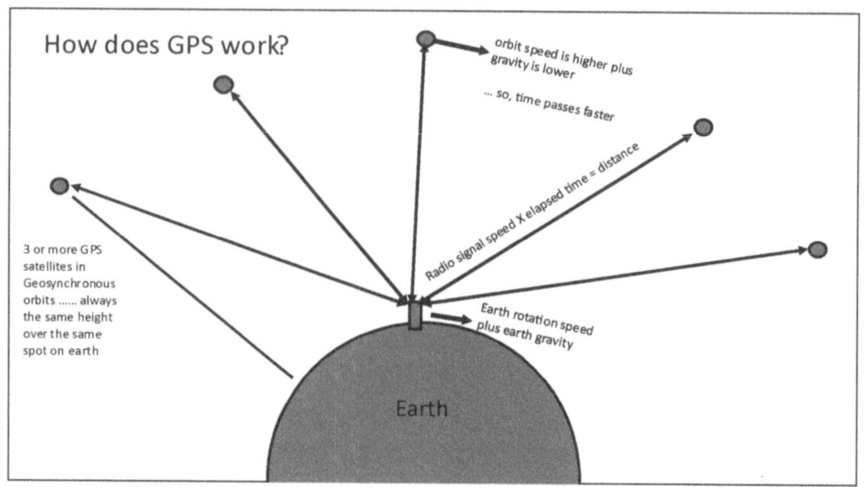

Given this, it is critical that when the satellite sends a signal telling the "satellite time" when the signal was sent, and the receiver on earth receives the signal at "earth time", then the two clocks must be continuously resynchronized. If not, the error in the calculated position on Earth can be as much as 5 miles per day. The designers of the system had to include a correction factor for the time dilation. (Google "time dilation effect on GPS system" for more information)

Even though it sounds like science fiction, it is a known fact that time passes at different rates for different observers. With God, Scripture says that a thousand years are as a day gone by (Psalms 90:4, 2Peter 3:8). Science says time is flexible. So, **Scripture and science tell the same story of creation (1).**

So, if (since) God is omnipresent, or present everywhere in the universe at once, and if (since) He is eternal, what is His time compared to ours? Is the time that looks like a billion years to us just a workday for an eternal God? Is the discussion of the length of a creation day about as relevant as the Middle Ages debate over how many angels can dance on the head of a pin?

Chapter 16:
Creation Day One

The first three words in scripture are "In the beginning" (Genesis 1:1). Already, **<u>Scripture and science tell the same story of origins (2)</u>**. Both now say there was a beginning.

In the mid-20th century, Edwin Hubble discovered with measurements that every galaxy in the universe is moving away from every other galaxy. That means that the universe is expanding. Imagine a balloon with dots painted on it. As you inflate the balloon, each dot moves farther away from all of the other dots. If I reverse the process and deflate the balloon, the dots move closer together again. If you make a video or a computer model of the expanding universe, then run that video/model in reverse for 13.8 billion years, the dots all move together to a point, and you arrive at a beginning where the entire universe is the size of a single proton, or smaller. This tiny spot of energy is what scientists call a singularity. This is the basis for the Big Bang theory. Note that the Big Bang theory has nothing to do with the evolution of species. It is the physics of the origins of inanimate materials and forces.

Until Edwin Hubble discovered that the universe is expanding, and the Big Bang theory was developed in the mid-20th century, the conventional wisdom among scientists was that the universe was eternal and unchanging. It had no beginning and no progression of changes. This concept goes at least as far back as the Greek philosophers. Today, due to the Big Bang concept, conventional wisdom among scientists is that the universe had a beginning, and it is constantly changing.

Note that for decades after Edwin Hubble's discovery, some scientists struggled to find a viable theory that eliminated the need for a beginning. Why? First, if there was a beginning, there must have been a cause for that beginning. Second, if there was a beginning some 13.8 billion years ago, the universe has not existed for enough time for all of the life forms and all of the inanimate materials to have developed through purely natural processes. In short, if there was a beginning, there must have been a God, a transcendent, intelligent, powerful being, who started it all. Even today, some scientists resist the concept of a beginning because they do not want to accept the existence of a transcendent creator God. However, the measured scientific data is pretty conclusive. There was a beginning.

Again, note that many like to claim that the Big Bang concept eliminates the need for a creator god. Does it? I think the clear answer is no, it does not. Consider this:

1. The Big Bang says that all of the matter and energy in the universe started as a singularity of infinitely dense pure raw energy. However, science has no viable theory for where that singularity came from. Dare I say the creator God provided the singularity??

2. The Big Bang says that at some point, the singularity started to inflate and expand into our universe. However, Science has no viable idea for what caused the singularity to start to inflate. Again, dare I say the creator God decided to start the process??

3. The Big Bang says that the inflation rate of the universe had to be extremely precise to give us the exact proportions of particle forms and energy forms that give us the universe

we have today. In fact, one famous scientist has said that if the expansion rate of the early universe were a millionth of a percent faster or slower, our universe would never have developed. However, scientists have no idea why that rate was so precise. Scripture says, "The spirit of God moved." Dare I say that the creator God managed the precision??

4. The Big Bang says that the process that developed our universe was controlled by the laws of physics as we know them today. However, they have no idea how those laws of physics developed from nothing. Once again, dare I say that the laws of physics were commanded by the creator God??

Moving on, next, the Scriptures say in Hebrews 11:3 that God made that which is seen from that which is not seen. From this, Bible scholars have gotten the concept of creation "ex nihilo," or from nothing. Science says that the universe started from a singularity where all of the material and energy of the universe was concentrated into a ball of pure raw energy smaller than a single proton. It was infinitely dense. Note that science cannot deal with "nothing," and it cannot deal with infinity. The mathematics of science breaks down at zero and at infinity. Because of that, they theorize a singularity that is extremely close to zero or nothing. If you accept that a minuscule singularity of pure raw energy, the size of a single proton, is "that which is not seen," then **Scripture and science tell the same story of origins (3)**. Also, if the singularity was pure raw energy, it would be unseen. You cannot see energy. You cannot see gravity or electricity, magnetism, or any form of energy. You only see the effects of the energy.

Scripture does one better than science on the subject of "nothing." Science has no reasonable theory for where the singularity came from or why it started to expand or inflate. Creationists find it easy to see an infinite God as both the source of the singularity and the will that decided to make it inflate. If you are an atheist/Darwinist, you must believe that everything came from nothing, totally naturally, with no direction, and no cause or purpose. Which belief takes more faith?

Next, Scriptures say in Psalms 104:2 and other places that God stretched out the heavens. Science says that the universe started as a singularity smaller than a single proton and inflated into the universe we have today. "Stretched out" and "inflated" sound like different words that describe the same event or action. **<u>Once again, Scripture and science tell the same story of origins (4)</u>**.

Next, scripture says in Genesis 1:2 that in the beginning the earth (the physical realm) was without form and void. Science says that in the earliest moments of the inflation of the universe, the only thing that existed was pure raw energy. With only energy, it had no structure, no form, and no solid materials, no atoms, nor even subatomic particles. With no atoms of any kind, it was "void" or empty. It could easily be described as without form and void. Even after simple atoms started to form, they would have had no structure and no features, just a cloud of loose atoms, so the universe would still be without form and void. Again, **<u>Scripture and science tell the same story of origins (5)</u>**.

Some people read "without form and void" to mean that planet Earth was created first and is described as being featureless with no mountains, rivers, oceans, etc., and devoid of any life. However, that doesn't seem to fit with the rest of the scripture narrative. Also, if you get online and look at NASA pictures of dust clouds in space, what scientists call the pillars of creation, you see that you could easily describe them as "without form and void." The cover photo on this book is just one of many such pictures.

As I said earlier, several ancient cultures had creation stories that describe an initial state of chaos that was made orderly by the action of a god. Again, if you accept the old adage that where there is smoke, there must be fire, then the agreement among these ancient creation accounts seems to indicate that they all had some common revelation from God that was handed down from antiquity.

Next, Scriptures say in Genesis 1:2 that the spirit of God hovered or moved over the "waters," or some translations say the "deep". What waters? Science says that as the Big Bang started to inflate, it started to cool off, and sub-atomic particles started to "condense" out of the pure raw energy of the singularity. When all material was sub-atomic particles, before any atoms formed, it was in what science calls a quantum state. That quantum state has both wave properties and particle properties. In other words, it has fluid properties. Imagine a body of water where energy moves in a stream like particles, but it also moves in waves. This is a simple description of a quantum state of matter.

Quantum physics is the branch of physics that deals with sub-atomic particles. I don't understand quantum physics very well (not many people do), but I have read one author who says that the term "waters" in Genesis 1:2 is a good description of the initial fluid quantum state of matter. Quantum physicists call this early pool of subatomic particles the Dirac sea. Another author says the "first matter in the universe may have been a perfect liquid"

(Google that phrase). Since ancient Hebrew had no words for quantum properties, what better describes a fluid condition, a perfect liquid, than the word "waters." Once again, different words describe the same condition. If you can accept that interpretation, then **<u>Scripture and science tell the same story of origins</u>" (6)**.

The significance of the Spirit of God hovering or moving over the "waters" of the quantum cloud/pool of subatomic particles is pretty important. Science tells us that within that cloud/pool (the Dirac sea), both the number of distinct subatomic particles and the mix or ratio or percentage of each particle's quantity to the whole became very precisely what was needed to form the universe that we have today and make it suitable for human life. In fact, scientists have identified hundreds of physical constants that developed in the first moments of the universe that are just right to make a universe that supports life. Even small deviations in any one of these constants would make life impossible. Scientists have no explanation for how these precise values came to be except to say that the rate of inflation of the universe had to be extremely precise within a very narrow range. That level of precision is way beyond the possibility of natural or "accidental" processes. The Bible explains it, saying that before any atoms existed, the Spirit of God was directing, managing, and designing all the precision necessary to build our universe.

Not only does science not know where the singularity came from or why it started to inflate, but it also has no idea why it developed with just the exact features needed to form our universe. Science recognizes the extreme fine-tuning of many variables as being what makes our universe suitable to support life. There are hundreds of physical values from the gravitational constant to the electrical charge on an electron, and hundreds more that must be what they are today within a fraction of a fraction of a percent. However, scientists have no theory for how those variables came to have this razor's edge of precise values needed to form our universe. Scripture says the Spirit of God "hovered" over the early creation, presumably making it develop precisely as needed.

So, science says the early universe had to develop very precise values of many physical constants, and scripture says the spirit of God was managing the process. **<u>Once again, it sounds like science and scripture agree(30).</u>**

Atheistic scientists have gone through some pretty convoluted philosophical and intellectual gyrations to try to figure out how the original condition of quantum matter developed into our universe by totally natural materialistic methods. They have made some very strong claims for some of their theories, and some have gained popular support, but in the end, they fail to answer the question of how the universe arose. In spite of their claims, they have not eliminated the need for a creator.

Next, Scriptures tell us in Genesis 1:3 that as the final event of Day One, God said, "Let there be light." Science tells us that light is a component of the electromagnetic force (EMF), one of the four basic forces in the universe (see chapter 9). Light is electromagnetic radiation. We think of light as the visible rainbow spectrum of light, but it is much more than that. We know that infrared light is invisible light beyond one end of the scale of light frequencies/colors (the rainbow), and ultraviolet light is invisible light beyond the other end of that scale.

Electromagnetic radiation or "light" also includes radio waves, microwaves, gamma rays, x-rays, and much more. We don't often think of light as being the same basic force as electricity and magnetism, but science says it is. Most people today don't recognize that almost all of the electricity in our grid is generated when magnetic fields inside a rotating generator shaft are managed in such a way as to generate electricity. So, since ancient Hebrew had no words for electricity or magnetism or radiation, God inspired Moses to say God created light, which signifies the EMF force. Anyone can understand "light", but even today, not many understand EMF.

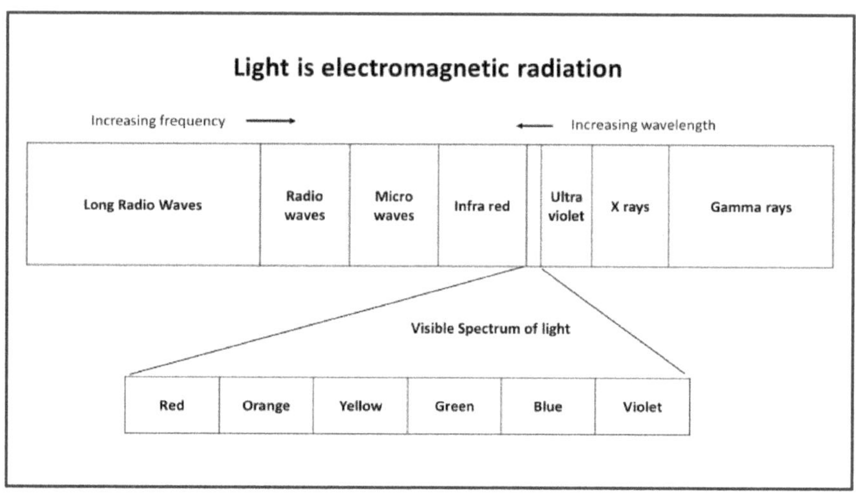

Science says that EMF appeared early in the Big Bang sequence, but after subatomic particles appeared and after the strong nuclear force had pulled those particles together to form atomic nuclei. Scripture says God created EMF in that same sequence that science has found. So, **Scripture and science tell the same story of origins" (7)**.

EMF has one other important function. EMF is the basic "glue" that holds electrons in orbits around atomic nuclei to make atoms possible. Without the EMF, all there would be is a soup of atomic nuclei, but no atoms. So, at the end of Day one, all of the quantum fluid pool of subatomic particles had been created from the pure raw energy of the singularity, and all of the forces had been created to make atoms possible. What existed at the end of Day One was a chaotic universe full of simple atoms, mostly Hydrogen plus some Helium, in a cloud that was without form and void.

So, EMF appeared early in the Big Bang sequence, but after the 17 subatomic particles and the strong nuclear force had created atomic nuclei, now there was EMF to hold electrons in orbit around those nuclei, so now simple atoms existed. Scripture has no word for atoms, so it doesn't directly say that no atoms existed until after God said, "Let there be light", but it says nothing about basic materials until discussing solid ground and seas on day three. So, like science, Scripture says nothing about solid materials until after day one, after EMF or light was created, so **<u>Scripture and science tell the same story of origins</u>" (8)**.

When God said, "Let there be light," He created not only our visible light, but the whole spectrum of electromagnetic radiation, plus the electric and the magnetic forces, and the atoms themselves. When we warm our hands by a campfire, that energy is EMF. When we cook our food, that energy is EMF. When we turn on an electric light bulb, that energy is EMF. When we charge up our cell phone, that energy is EMF. God said, "Let there be light," and created all of these forms of energy. Quite a job.

Also, note that without light, there would be no means of communication. Most of our modern communication electronics use light or EMF in their various forms. Radio, television, internet, computers, fiber optics, etc., all function with EMF/light. Light is often used as a metaphor for communication and learning. Scripture often refers to people who are walking in the light as people who are walking in communion with God. Those who are without light, in darkness, have no communion with God. Challenge: Are you walking in the light?

Some folks believe that since God is described elsewhere in scripture as being a God of light, that light existed before the beginning, and at this point, God simply removed a barrier and made His light visible on the earth. Once again, this assumes that planet Earth was created first, which doesn't seem to fit the rest of the creation story. It also assumes that God is composed of photons like the light He created on Day One. I expect that when God is described as being a God of "light," it is referring to His holiness, His righteousness, His wisdom, and other positive spiritual properties. I doubt that it is saying God is composed of photons. Or physical light.

Chapter 17:
Creation day two

Scientists tell us that most of the events of day one most likely happened in a fraction of a second. However, they also say it took several million years before the inflation of the universe matured and reached a point where it had cooled enough for atoms to exist. However long it took, by the end of day one, we had a rapidly inflating/expanding soup/cloud/chaos of mostly simple hydrogen atoms (one proton & one electron). Please note that not only do science and scripture agree on this, but some of the ancient creation myths from other cultures also describe the earth or universe being made orderly out of an original chaos.

In Genesis 1:6-7, Scripture tells us that on day two, God separated the waters above from the waters below. Many people interpret that to mean that God created clouds and rain in what is called a hydrologic cycle on planet Earth, but that doesn't seem basic enough to merit a whole day of creation. It also seems out of sequence if God created oceans on day three. I ask myself, "What basic feature did God need to create to separate heavy liquid water below from light water vapor above?" Then it dawned on me, the thing that separates heavy materials from light materials is the force of gravity, another of the four basic forces in the universe (see Chapter 9).

On day two, God created gravity. However, since the ancient Hebrew language had no word for gravity, it was described by one of its features. It separates light and heavy materials. Gravity was not identified by scientists until Isaac Newton in the seventeenth century, some 400 years ago, and nearly 3000 years after Moses wrote Genesis. The original audience for the creation story was a world 3500 years ago, where people had no concept of the force of gravity. In order for God to communicate the creation of gravity to them, and us, He had to use something that they would recognize. Separating liquid water from clouds (water vapor) effectively communicates the effects of gravity.

Given the audience, the story is written in such a manner that it was scientifically accurate, but at the same time communicated God's power in a way that told the original audience that God made clouds and rain, so they were not gods in and of themselves. The story is written in a way that communicates a message to the ancients but also in a way that is scientifically accurate so that even 21st-century scientists can recognize the truth.

Science says that the force of gravity had to develop some time after the inflation of the universe had reached a point where it would continue to expand in spite of the pull of gravity. If the gravity developed too soon, it would have pulled all of those newly formed atoms back into the singularity. The universe would have collapsed back into a singularity. Scripture says gravity was created on day two, which is some amount of time after atoms with mass were created on day one. Whether you believe that amount of time was billions of years or mere hours, once again, **<u>Scripture and science tell the same story of origins (9).</u>**

Gravity is one of those things that we take for granted and never think about what it means. In addition to holding our feet on the ground, gravity is the force that holds the moon in orbit around the Earth. It holds the Earth in orbit around the sun. It holds the sun in orbit around the center of the Milky Way galaxy.

In the earliest days of the universe, gravity was the force that pulled small clumps of hydrogen atoms out of the shapeless cloud into larger and larger clumps/concentrations, which became celestial bodies that became stars and planets. Between those clumps of gas, open space started to appear. Scripture calls that open space a firmament. Gravity pulled order out of the chaos and made the universe and our solar system what we see today. It brought order to the chaos.

Note that the force of gravity is one of those physical constants that has to be precisely what it is today in order for the universe to become suitable for life to exist. The Spirit of God hovered over the waters, the newly forming universe, and made it so.

Gravity was created from nothing and makes the universe what it is today. How awesome is our God?

Chapter 18:
Creation day three

In Genesis 1:9, Scripture says that day three of creation begins with God creating dry land and oceans. That action suggests two things had to happen. First, God had to create rocks and water. Until this point, the creation narrative says nothing about solid, dense, heavy materials.

Some suggest that verse 1 of Genesis, "In the beginning God created the heavens and the earth," says that God created the planet Earth first. I would submit that this phrase in verse 1 serves as a summary statement, which is then followed by a more detailed explanation. I am also convinced that the intended meaning of the verse is that God created the spirit realm, which is called "heavens," and the physical realm, which is called "earth." Given that interpretation, what we have at the end of day two is huge masses of small atoms like hydrogen and helium being pulled together and compressed into huge balls of gas by gravity, but we have none of the heavier elements like silicon, carbon, oxygen, iron, gold, and so on. These heavier elements are necessary to make solid land, and they are necessary to make water.

So, what is required to make dry land, or rocks, or water? Science tells us that the heavier elements are made when fusion reactions inside those huge balls of gravitationally compressed gas called stars "fuse" smaller atoms into larger atoms and give off energy in the form of heat and light. Fusion reactions are what make hydrogen bombs go bang. When the fusion reactions inside those huge balls of gas (stars) reach a climax, the star explodes as a supernova, spreading fragments of those heavy elements throughout the universe, where gravity pulls them together into planets, comets, meteors, and so on. So fusion reactions inside stars make heavy elements. These fusion reactions also make the stars shine and produce energy/light. In fact, it is the fusion reactions inside our star (the sun) that make it give us light and heat.

So, if fusion reactions inside the huge balls of gas pulled together by gravity (stars) create heavy elements, what causes fusion reactions? Those fusion reactions are caused by the weak nuclear force (see chapter 9). On day three, God created the weak nuclear force, the last of the four basic forces in the universe. So, **Scripture and science tell the same story of origins (10)**. After gravity, the weak nuclear force appeared/was created to form the heavier elements that make up land and water.

Those heavier elements that are created in the cores of stars then combine chemically to make water and rocks of various kinds. The Oxygen combines with hydrogen to make water. The Oxygen also combines with silicon, calcium, iron, and other elements to make rocks. Carbon combines with hydrogen to make all sorts of hydrocarbons. In short, we now have water and land.

Once we have water and rocks, God has to make those heavy rocks rise above the level of the lighter water to make "dry" land. So, what makes our continents, our dry land, rise above sea level? Why do we not have a planet with all of the heavy rocks at the center and all of the lighter water on top, covering the entire surface?

Science tells us that our continents are huge tectonic plates that float on a molten core of rocks and metals deep inside the Earth. As they float, they collide, causing some tectonic plates to rise above sea level while others are subducted below sea level. Those collisions also cause earthquakes and volcanic activity, which push rocks upward above sea level.

So, next, we have to ask, what causes the core of the Earth to remain molten to drive that tectonic activity? The pressure of gravity is certainly part of the formula, but by itself, it is not nearly enough to generate the heat needed to melt the rocks. There is some thought that some of the heat in the core of planet Earth is residual, or left over, from the formation of the planet. Mars and Venus are rocky planets like Earth, which undoubtedly also started their existence as molten balls of rock, but as far as we know, they don't have molten cores today. So, it appears that residual heat and gravity are not enough to keep the core of a planet molten for very long.

Science tells us that the radioactive decay of heavy isotopes of things like uranium and other materials in the Earth's core creates most of the heat to keep the core molten. This is the same radioactive decay process that makes storage of spent fuel from nuclear reactors difficult, since the residual radioactive decay makes it stay very hot for a very long time.

If fusion reactions in stars make the heavy materials that make up rocks and water, and if radioactive decay causes heat to keep the core of the Earth molten, then what causes fusion reactions and radioactive decay? The answer to both questions is the weak nuclear force. The last of the four basic forces in the universe (see chapter 9). On day three, God created the weak nuclear force, the last of the four basic forces in the universe. So,__ **Scripture and science tell the same story of origins (11)**. After gravity, the weak nuclear force appeared/was created.

At this point, all of the mechanisms to make all of the inanimate elements and forces, and to gather them into stars and planets, are now in place and ready for life to exist. Science agrees that before any life appeared, all of the inanimate materials and all of the basic forces existed. So, **Scripture and science tell the same story of origins (12)**.

So, on day three, God first made the heavy elements that make up land and water, plus all heavy elements for all planets in the whole universe. Then he made that land float on a core of molten magma, so it rose out of the water. By the end of day three, God had created the gravity that He used to pull balls of gas out of the chaos/cloud of small atoms, and He had created the mechanism for those balls of gas to react and send out dazzling light as well as the heavier elements of the universe. Once again, the glory of God is on display. How awesome is the Creator God?

This might be a good place to point out that both science and scripture agree that there has been a progression in the creation of our universe. All of the materials and forces had to be in place before life as we know it could appear. So, **Science and Scripture tell the same story of origins (13)**.

Chapter 19:
Creation day three - Life

In any discussion of creation, the second big gorilla in the room is often the subject of plant life creation and its location in the sequence of the story. A casual read of the story seems to indicate that mature complex plant life was created before the sun was created to energize those plants and before insects were created to pollinate them. The Sunday school picture story books often seem to show a planet Earth covered with mature, fruitful plants on day three.

For many years, scholars have recognized that the narrative of Genesis seems to put plant life in the wrong place. They have struggled to understand why God would have created mature plants before the environment was complete and ready to support them. The Young Earth Creation folks believe this proves a 24-hour creation day. They say that the days of Genesis must have been very short because plants were created before the sun was created to energize them and before insects were created to pollinate them.

These folks have interpreted the words of Genesis to mean that God spoke, and instantly the earth was covered with thick, lush, mature vegetation. While God is certainly capable of such a scenario, and He certainly could have done it that way, is that the only way He could have done it? Does the evidence that we see in God's creation tell us that He made all mature plants in a matter of hours, a few thousand years ago? Or does the evidence tell us that God created plant life and then developed the abundance and diversity that we see today by manipulating and managing a process over a period of thousands or even millions of years?

Allow me to propose a few thoughts that might challenge the YEC interpretation of this issue.

1) The scripture never specifically says if God individually created mature plants in all their diversity or if He created a simple microscopic alga and then directed a process of diversification that developed it into giant redwoods and everything in between. Also, ask yourself if God instantaneously created a world full of mature trees, did he create them with growth rings for years that never existed? Does that sound like a God of truth?

2) If God created the weak nuclear force at the beginning of day three, then the nuclear furnaces in trillions of stars blinked on. With those nuclear furnaces blazing, sunlight (starlight) existed early on day three to energize the photosynthesis that makes plants grow. Astronomers who have studied the inflation of the universe have said that when stars first started to form and first started to blink on their internal nuclear furnaces, they were not yet gathered into clusters that we call galaxies. Also, none of them were crushed into black holes, so there were trillions of times more stars than what we have today. Also, the universe was smaller (not yet fully inflated), so those stars were much closer together. The pattern of those stars would have been denser than what we see today. All stars would have been closer to Earth than they are today. If that many stars were evenly distributed in a dense pattern across the universe and closer to Earth, they estimate that the entire universe

would have been bathed in light that was possibly more intense than the sunlight that falls on Earth today. The sky of planet Earth would have been almost uniformly lit with intense starlight coming from all directions, possibly for 24 hours per day. In that case, no matter where in the universe plants were created, they would have had ample light to sustain photosynthesis. Also, that light would have been coming from all directions, so there was endless daylight across the whole globe of Earth. That might explain why we have huge fossil fuel deposits (decayed microscopic plant remains) in the Arctic and Antarctic. So, while God may have created everything in 24 hours, the sunlight argument does not prove that to be true.

3) The scripture narrative never specifically says that plants were created upon the earth (Gen 1:11). Since astronauts found living cells on the exterior surfaces of the space lab, there has been a growing theory that plant life might have begun somewhere else in the universe and was transported to Earth on meteors or comets. They call this theory "panspermia." Even if we allow that this might be true, it only relocates the question of first life from Earth to somewhere else. I mention this as food for thought. I doubt that God created plants on another planet and then transported them to Earth, but it is interesting to consider, and you can't rule it out.

4) As for the insect question, there are many plants that require no insects to pollinate them, and there are alternate methods of pollination for those plants that today depend largely on insects. I have seen tomatoes grown in screened-in greenhouses where there are no insects to pollinate them.

The operators of those greenhouses go around daily and touch each of the blossoms with a tuning fork to vibrate the pollen loose and pollinate the blossoms. If the first plants God created were microscopic plants that required no insects to pollinate them, then this would be very compatible with plants being created before insects. Likewise, God may have had alternate methods to pollinate plants in the days before insects were created. Oh, by the way, scripture never tells us specifically when insects were created. It is certainly possible that God also created insects on day three. So, while God may have created everything in days of 24-hour duration, the insect argument does not prove that to be true.

5) If God created plant life before He had created all of the environment necessary for those plants to thrive, it seems to suggest that God made a mistake in the sequencing of creation. Did He create plants before He was ready for them? I just don't see that as a slam-dunk proof of six short 24-hour days of creation. My God just doesn't make mistakes.

6) When looking at the Scripture account of plants, you need to remember that only mature plants are mentioned because these are what the local cultures of the day worshiped. God is saying that plants are not worthy of worship; only the God who created them is worthy of worship.

7) When looking at the Scripture account of plants, you also need to remember that the original audience for the story would not have recognized the existence of microscopic life forms since the microscope had not yet been invented.

If the creation of plant life on day three refers to the creation of microscopic plant forms to be followed by more complex and diverse plant forms later, then the sequence would make sense.

So, why does the Scripture narrative put plants on day three? I see two possible reasons. First, I think it is most likely that the creation of plants on day three is related to the creation of the weak nuclear force earlier on day three. The weak nuclear force led to nuclear fusion in the stars, which led to the sunlight/starlight necessary to support photosynthesis. The chemical process of photosynthesis is the very base of the food chain for all life. Plants convert sunlight into materials that provide the food for all animal life. Plants convert the inanimate materials created so far into food for the creatures God will create later. Once you have photosynthesis and light from any source, you can have plants, whether they are located on planet Earth or elsewhere, and whether they are single cells or mature trees.

Second, while I don't understand all of the science, I have read that plants, especially microscopic plants, with photosynthesis are/were a significant facilitator in the process of plate tectonics, which gave us our continents and dry land. Somehow, they change the chemistry of not only the air, but also the water, soil, and rocks in such a way that tectonic activity is maintained. It seems that plant photosynthesis creates the chemicals that lubricate the fault lines so tectonic activity can proceed. Assuming that to be true, then the creation of microscopic plants on day three was instrumental in making dry land appear and separating the dry land from the oceans.

Now, let's get to the real issue with plant creation. In Genesis 1:11, Scripture tells us that during the period of time referred to as "day three," God created the first living organisms. Until the middle of day three, scripture has only referenced inanimate materials. At the end of day three, all of the physical materials and forces have been created to make up the bodies of living things. At this point, God starts to create things that can absorb energy, absorb nutrients, grow, and reproduce more of their own kind. In short, He creates the first living organisms.

Scripture tells us that the first living organisms created were plants. Scripture does not mention microscopic organisms of any kind. An audience 3000+ years ago would not have grasped the significance because, without microscopes, they knew nothing of microscopic life. Science tells us that the first living organisms were microscopic plants with photosynthesis that absorbed and sequestered carbon from the atmosphere and released oxygen into the atmosphere to form the mix of elements that are in our air today. So, both science and scripture tell us that the first living things were plants. So, once again, **Scripture and science tell the same story of origins (14)**.

Let me qualify that last paragraph. Some scientists will tell you that animal life appeared first, then plant life. However, you need to be careful. When they say that, they are referring to complex plant life with woody stems. There are fossils of microscopic plant life forms much older than the earliest known animals.

In fact, science tells us that the first plant life was microscopic cyanobacteria or simple plants, which do not require intense sunlight nor insects to pollinate them. Things like algae, mosses, and ferns were the first forms of plant life. These plant forms could easily have flourished on a planet illuminated only by intense starlight and devoid of insects. Scripture refers to fully mature trees with flowers and fruit bearing seeds, but it does not give us any details about any progression of plant complexity. It seems entirely reasonable and logical to conclude that on day three, God created simple plant life before the solar system was stabilized to provide regular cycles of sunlight. Then He continued a process of increasing plant complexity in parallel with the development of our solar system on day four, plus other life forms on days five and six.

Scripture says that God is the author of life. Science says that the amazing complexity of even a simple single-cell organism makes it statistically impossible for life to have spontaneously generated (see chapter 11). If the first life could only have happened by supernatural (not random natural/accidental) means, then **<u>Scripture and science tell the same story of origins (15)</u>**.

The bottom line here is that at the end of the time period known as "day three," God created the first living organisms, which were plants.

Chapter 20:
Creation Day four

Science has evidence that our solar system was formed about 9 billion years after the beginning of the Big Bang. In the early years of our solar system, the orbits of planets were chaotic, and collisions were common. Our planet, and indeed our solar system, began to take its current shape about 5 billion years ago.

Scripture says that the relationship between the earth, sun, moon, planets, and other stars was established on Day Four, three days after the beginning. Whether you believe it happened in three days or billions of years, our solar system did not exist at the beginning. It was formed some amount of time after the beginning. Therefore, once again, **Scripture and science tell the same story of origins (16).**

Many people read the account of Day Four "literally" and conclude that God instantaneously created from nothing the sun, moon, planets, and other stars surrounding a pre-existing earth on Day Four. However, a careful reading of the narrative (Gen 1:16) finds that on Day Four God <u>caused</u> the greater light to <u>rule (regulate)</u> the day and the lesser light to <u>rule (regulate)</u> the night. The emphasis seems to be on creating a system to regulate time. In other words, a clock and a calendar.

Scientists today believe there was a time when the orbits of the planets around our sun were chaotic. There were collisions and destruction on a wide scale. They believe that at one point, another small planet, named Theia, collided with the Earth, and the debris from that collision collected together to form our moon. It seems those conditions would not have made for a very reliable clock or calendar. It follows that Day Four is when God stabilized our solar system.

Scientists searching for habitable, earth-like planets around other stars have found that they are extremely rare. In fact, they have discovered that the natural birth process for a star system begins with a cloud of dust and gases that rotates and is drawn together by gravity. The normal natural progression, controlled by the laws of physics, makes it nearly impossible to have a rocky planet like Earth sitting in the Goldilocks Zone (not too hot and not too cold) around a star like our sun. Day Four is the point where God may have supernaturally managed the birth of our unique solar system from a cloud of dust and gases, giving it just the right combination of features necessary to make a planet suitable for life.

I recently watched a science TV show about the birth of our solar system. In the course of a one-hour show, they used the term "luck" so many times I lost count. Every time one of the scientists explained some unique feature of our planet and our solar system that made Earth habitable, they would comment about how lucky we were. I might believe in luck or chance once or twice, but not dozens or hundreds of times. It seems our solar system required supernatural action to make it unique among star systems and suitable for life.

Knowing what we know today about the movements of heavenly bodies, I understand the Scripture narrative to mean that on Day Four God established the orbits of the various objects in our solar system in such a way that we would have a heavenly clock, along with regular repeating day and night cycles to regulate life on earth.

Scripture further indicates that God established the relationship between the earth and all of the trillions of galaxies and other stars for the purpose of determining times and seasons. The sun and moon rule or regulate the day and night cycles, giving us a heavenly clock, and the rest of the stars indicate times and seasons to give us a calendar.

Humans have, for millennia, studied the stars to determine times and seasons. One classic example is the Mayan Calendar, which is known to have been very precise. The ancient Chinese, the builders of Stonehenge, and other ancient cultures also had very precise calendars based on the stars. Today, scientists use sophisticated and powerful telescopes to study the stars. What they measure leads them to conclude that the "beginning" happened about 13.8 billion years ago. So, if the stellar calendar that God gave us tells us the beginning was 13.8 billion years ago, why do some of us not believe it?

One speculation says that Day Four might also be understood as the point where God created time itself. If God existed before the beginning, then He existed before time and space. This means that at some point, time had to be created. We commonly think of time being created simultaneously with the beginning of space and matter. We also know from proven scientific studies that time dilation (see chapter 16) exists, and that with God, a day is as a thousand years and a thousand years is as a day. So, if God created time and set the dimensions of time, we might understand Day Four as the point in the creation sequence where that happened. I think this is probably not the meaning of Day Four, but it is interesting to consider.

Another speculation says that Day Four might be the time when God created the substance scientists call dark matter (see chapter 9). The gravity produced by dark matter has a tremendous influence on the movements of all heavenly bodies. If Day Four is the point where God established the relationships between planet Earth and all of the other heavenly bodies, it could also be the point where He created dark matter and distributed it in a precise pattern so that its gravity would regulate the motions of heavenly bodies in our solar system. As I said, it is speculation.

I have one final comment about Day Four. For millennia, men have worshiped the sun and the moon. Here God is declaring that these heavenly bodies were placed in our sky by Him and are not themselves gods. The sun and moon are not worthy of worship, but the God who created them and set them in their courses is worthy of worship. While those heavenly bodies are awesome, when we study the sun, the moon, and the universe full of trillions of stars, it should fill us with a sense of awe for the Creator who built them, not for the objects themselves.

Chapter 21:
Creation Day five

Scripture says that the next event in the sequence of creation was marine life (Gen 1:20). Science says animal life began in the oceans. **Science and Scripture tell the same story of origins (17).**

Also, on Day Five, after marine creatures, Scripture says God created creatures that fly through the air (Gen 1:20b). Again, science says that birds appeared on planet earth after marine life had appeared. **Science and Scripture tell the same story of origins (18).**

I ask myself, "What is common among swimming, water-breathing creatures and air-breathing creatures that fly through the air? How are they different from land-dwelling, air-breathing creatures created later?" Also, which is which? Why are there two separate days of creation, one for sea and air creatures and one later for land-dwelling creatures? Then it occurs to me that the most obvious common feature for birds and fish is that they reproduce by laying eggs and hatching them outside the body. On the other hand, the distinctive feature for land creatures (mammals and marsupials) is that they reproduce by developing a fetus in a womb and giving birth. While there may be exceptions, the broad general concept seems to be egg-hatching creatures first on Day Five and placental or birthing creatures later on Day Six.

The Bible does not tell us when insects, spiders, worms, and many other creatures were created. However, if we apply the egg-laying description, it is easy to place them early with the fish and birds. It also does not tell us when amphibians, reptiles, and dinosaurs were created, but once again, applying the egg-laying description places most of them early in the sequence of animal life appearing on earth. Science puts them between marine creatures and birds. On the other hand, air-breathing sea mammals such as whales, dolphins, and seals would have been created later when land-dwelling mammals were created. Again, science agrees that marine mammals came after land mammals.

Science tells us that the first life to appear was microscopic plant life, then simple animal life, then more complex animal life. Darwinists speculate that animal life appeared and diversified over a period of many billions of years. However, fossils show the progression of simple to more complex egg-laying animal life concentrated in a much shorter period called the Cambrian explosion of life. Instead of multiple billions of years, the fossils show the appearance of egg-laying creatures concentrated in just a few million years. In geologic terms, this is very quick and very recent, thus an "explosion" of new life forms.

During this Cambrian explosion of new life forms, almost all of the known families of egg-laying creatures "suddenly" appear in the fossil record. By "suddenly," I not only mean that it happened in a short time span, but also that they do not seem to have previous life forms that they evolved from. It also means that there have not been new creatures appearing after that event. It seems to have been a distinct event, not an ongoing process. That event may have lasted millions of years, but it ended at some point and no new egg-laying life forms have appeared since. Many have become extinct, but no new ones have appeared.

So, science says all the known egg-laying creatures first appeared quickly, after plants appeared and before birthing animals appeared. Scripture says it all happened on Day Five. Once again, **Scripture and science tell the same story of origins (19).**

It is interesting to note that no new families, types, or kinds of egg-laying creatures have been discovered by science after the Cambrian explosion of life. Many creatures whose fossils appear in the Cambrian period have become extinct, but no new ones have appeared. It seems that whatever was causing this wild proliferation of new creatures stopped at some point. Scripture says that at the end of Day Five God surveyed what He had created and called it "good." If we understand "good" as meaning it was complete and no new egg-laying creatures were created after Day Five, then **Scripture and science tell the same story of origins (20).**

As I noted in an earlier chapter, the Bible does not give us a lot of details about the creation. It gives us a broad outline. The broad outline may not answer all our questions, but it is enough to show us that God's Word is accurate and true. It is enough to allow us to study the created world and know that there exists a Creator God.

I have found an interesting side note regarding the progression of animal life creation. One author I have read said that marine creatures have about 150 different types of cells in their bodies. Think skin cells, muscle cells, brain cells, and so forth. Birds and amphibians have about 200 different types of cells, and mammals have about 250 types of cells. The progression follows a pattern of increasing complexity as laid out in Scripture. Hmmmmm.

Chapter 22:
Creation Day six

Scripture says that on Day Six, after all the egg-laying creatures had been created, God created land animals (Gen 1:24). I understand this to mean all the creatures that breathe air and reproduce by giving birth and nursing their young with milk (mammals and marsupials). Since Scripture is not a science textbook, it does not give us a long list of animals created on Day Six, but it does provide some broad categories. There were domestic and wild animals, carnivores and herbivores, small and large, and everything in between. Once again, it is important to note that the animals specifically mentioned were animals that various pagan cultures worshipped. God is saying that the animals are not gods worthy of worship, but that the one true God who created them is worthy of worship.

Why God chose to separate the creation of the egg-laying and birthing creatures into two creation episodes is a mystery to me. Is there some fundamental difference in the DNA or the spirits or souls of these classes of creatures? I do not know.

Science says that mammals appeared and proliferated in a short period of geologic time soon after the extinction event that killed off the dinosaurs. Scripture calls it "Day Six." Once again, **Scripture and science tell the same story of origins (21).**

Science says that while the first small mammals may have existed alongside the dinosaurs, it was not until after the meteor strike that wiped out the dinosaurs that mammals proliferated quickly both in numbers and diversity. Dinosaurs are not mentioned in Scripture because they were extinct by the time the Scriptures were written. The audience for the story would not have understood what a dinosaur was. Also, no one was worshiping dinosaurs, so it was not necessary to emphasize that they were created creatures and not gods.

In both the case of egg-laying creatures and the case of birthing creatures, God commanded them to "be fruitful and multiply" (Gen 1:22). I see two possible understandings of that command. One could be to multiply in numbers of individuals in each species, family, or kind. The other would be to multiply in the diversity of species, families, or kinds. Either way, it appears that God did not instantaneously create a world full of fully mature and fully diversified animal life.

Now we need to ask, "Once God created the first living creature, what mechanism could He have used to diversify that population into the amazing collection of creatures that have ever lived, whether current or extinct?" The theistic evolutionists believe that God created the first life with the capability to evolve and diversify naturally. Once He made the first life, they believe God allowed natural evolution to create diverse species. Somehow, I have trouble believing that God left anything to chance or accident. However, could it be possible that God directed and used a supernaturally guided evolution? Could God have supernaturally made a frog to hatch from a fish egg? Or could He have made an eagle to hatch from a chicken egg? Could He have made a squirrel to be born to a chipmunk? While I reject the accidental diversification proposed by Darwinists and theistic evolutionists, I will keep an open mind on the possibility of a supernaturally guided progression of increasingly complex creatures. Scripture simply does not give us that level of detail.

Is it also possible that God created directly from dirt or mud a mature mating pair of each of the millions of kinds of creatures in the universe and then commanded them to fill the earth with their own kind? Of course, that is possible, but is that the only possibility allowed by a reasonable interpretation of Scripture? Whatever process God used, it appears that during the creation event, there was a supernatural process of some kind in operation. We do not know what it was simply because we do not see it in operation today. We can only guess at the process God used to multiply the diversity of creatures.

However, God reached a point where diversification was complete, and He commanded all creatures to reproduce according to their own kinds and only according to their own kinds. As with marine life, the fossil record shows the same story. Diversification of mammalian creatures increased rapidly up to a point, then it stabilized, and diversification stopped. After that point, all we see is extinctions, not new creatures. **<u>Scripture and science tell the same story of origins (22).</u>**

Darwinism speculates that many small mutations plus natural selection have given us the amazing diversity of living and extinct creatures. However, true science says that naturally occurring mutations in DNA are almost always neutral or harmful to the survivability of the creature. When you mutate the computer program of the cell, it has bad consequences.

Let me try an illustration. When I went to college back in the dark ages, I had one computer programming class. In those days, the only computer on campus was a huge machine in the business office and it had only limited capabilities. You programmed that machine by entering your commands on punch cards, which you arranged in a card deck in a specific sequence. There was a card reader that then read the cards in their proper sequence and entered your program into the computer. The problem was that if you accidentally lost a card or moved a card to a new place in your card deck (mutated the deck), it totally messed up your program. Now imagine a DNA molecule with a long string of protein sequences that are the computer code of the cell. A mutation that changes one of those proteins seems like it would be analogous to me losing one of the cards in my deck or damaging one of the cards. The program does not work when you do that.

Now reference the fruit fly studies mentioned earlier. Over 100 years of studies with fruit flies have given thousands of generations of fruit flies. In all those generations, scientists have seen amazing variations. None of them provided a net benefit to the fruit flies, and none of them created a new species. All were still fruit flies. All of the variation possibilities already existed within the fruit fly DNA. DNA mutations do not create new classes of creatures. God said diversity of kinds is complete. **<u>Scripture and science tell the same story of origins (22).</u>**

While we are all familiar with DNA, what we often do not recognize is that DNA does not determine basic body structures. Something called GRN, or Gene Regulating Networks, determines whether you have two legs plus two arms, or two legs plus two wings, or four legs with claws, or four legs with hooves, and so on. To get a new creature, the GRN would need to mutate. The GRN and its relationship to DNA is not well understood, but it is known to be extremely complex. The problem is that it is not clear to me that GRN mutations can create a stronger creature. Once again, as with DNA, natural mutations tend to almost exclusively make weaker creatures.

Whatever mechanism God used to proliferate the numbers of species, genus, families, or kinds in the mammalian world, He reached a point where it was complete. No new families, genus, or kinds of creatures appeared after that. Science also says that at some point, the progression of new creatures stopped. Today, while some new creatures have been discovered, there is no evidence that they have never existed before. Many creatures have become extinct, but no new previously nonexistent ones have appeared. **<u>Scripture and science tell the same story of origins (22).</u>**

Chapter 23:
Creation - Man

Scripture indicates that after creating all the other animals, God created man (Gen 1:26 & 27). According to the Bible, humans were the last creatures created. According to science, humans (Homo sapiens) were the last creatures to appear on earth. So, **Scripture and science tell the same story of origins (23).**

Scripture says that God created man from the dust of the earth (Gen 2:7). The common mental picture is that of an almighty God playing in the mud to make a statue of a man and then giving it mouth-to-mouth to breathe into it the breath of life. Somehow, I think that the dust of the earth is simply a metaphorical way to say that man was created with a body made up of the physical materials God had earlier created. Presumably, this distinguishes man from the angelic beings who do not have bodies made from the dust of the earth, meaning the physical materials of the universe.

The truly unique feature of man is not that he was made from the physical elements nor that he has the breath of life. Other animals have bodies composed of the physical elements of the universe and they have the breath of life. The standout feature of man is that he was created in the image of God (Gen 1:27). Scripture teaches us that God exists in three persons. God exists as Father, Son, and Holy Ghost. We humans also exist in three persons. We have body, mind, and spirit. We recognize our three persons when we say things like "my body does not want to do what my mind knows I should do" or "I do not feel like doing what I know I should do." When I say my mind knows I should do my homework, but my body does not feel like doing it, we have two persons of our being in conflict.

The relationship between our body and soul has been described as "I am my invisible soul, and I inhabit my body." My invisible soul lives in my physical body. So, I can say that I have never seen my wife of more than 50 years. I have never seen her invisible soul. I have only seen the physical body she inhabits. I may know the person she is because of our long relationship, so in that sense, I can know her soul, but I cannot physically see or touch her soul.

Note that as with God, where the Son and the Holy Spirit are subject to the will of the Father, we are also expected to have our bodies and our spirits subject to our minds. Christianity is not a religion for dummies. We are expected to fill our minds with the knowledge of God and to keep our bodies and emotions under the control of our minds. Is your mind being filled with the knowledge of God?

Humans are unique among animals in many ways. Science calls us Homo sapiens. Sapiens means "wise" or intelligent. We have the ability to think critically and abstractly. We have the ability to use complex language instead of grunts, squeals, and whistles. We have the capability to communicate in written languages. We have an amazing ability to learn from others. We have the ability to use tools. We build things. We are creative. We live in complex societies. We have characters capable of love, civility, selflessness, loyalty, and many other refined traits. We also have a conscience or a sense of right and wrong. Science has found these capabilities in no other creature, or at least not to nearly the same degree as they find them in humans or Homo sapiens. Scripture says we were created in the image of God. **<u>Scripture and science tell the same story of origins (25).</u>**

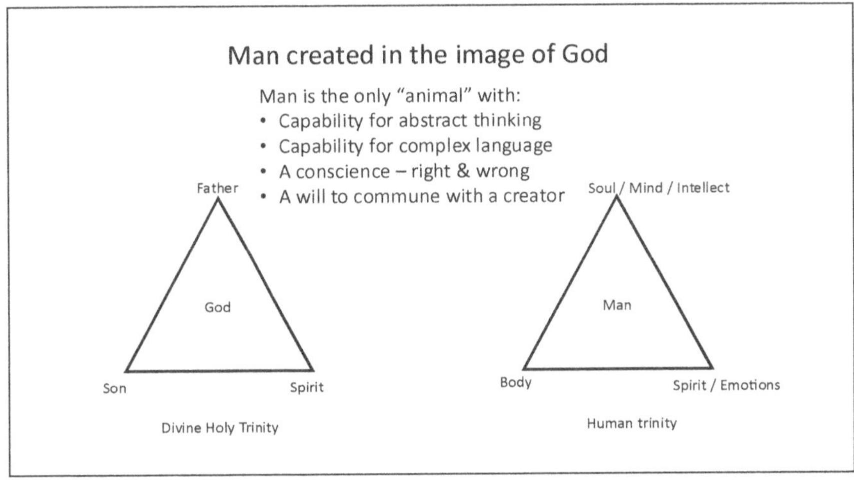

Perhaps our most unique feature is that we have a desire to worship a creator. Science has a lot of evidence of ancient human cultures worshipping some kind of god, but has found no other animal showing any desire to worship a higher supernatural being the way man does. Scripture says that Adam, the first human, walked and talked with God in the garden of Eden (Gen 3:8-9). He had fellowship with God. Once again, **<u>Scripture and science tell the same story of origins (26).</u>**

Note that science is confirming the existence of a human soul. In recent years, there has been an increase in documented cases of NDE (Near Death Experience). These are cases where the subject is clinically dead for several minutes or even hours. They have no heartbeat, no respiration, and no brain wave activity. Then after being dead for some period of time, they revive back to life. Note that they are not necessarily revived through medical intervention, but they frequently spontaneously revive. Interviews with hundreds or even thousands of these people have confirmed that there is a human consciousness that continues after death. This conscious being can apparently see, hear, smell, sense, and remember what is going on around them. These folks report being aware of what is happening not only in the room where their dead body is located but also in other nearby rooms. Some of them go a next step and leave the immediate vicinity, going to either a place they call heaven or a place they call hell. They give consistent detailed descriptions of both destinations. You would not expect hallucinations to have consistent stories among multiple people with multiple ethnic, cultural, and religious backgrounds. A detailed study is the subject of other books, but let me just say that both science and Scripture say that we have an existence apart from the body. We have a soul. Once again, **<u>Scripture and science tell the same story of origins (27).</u>**

Chapter 24:
Pre-Adamite creatures (Hominin)

Science tells us that they have evidence of creatures much like man existing on earth long before man appeared, but they have not found evidence of worship among those creatures. They are called hominin creatures. Note that there is some confusion between what science calls hominin and what they call hominid creatures. Hominid creatures are related to great apes and other primates. Hominin creatures are ancestors of modern humans. You have heard of Cro-Magnon man, Neanderthal man, and others. Science says that while these hominin creatures may have existed for many thousands of years, true humans, or Homo sapiens, those who show evidence of worshiping a god, have only existed for less than about 10 thousand years. Some allow up to about 30 to 50 thousand years ago for true human (Homo sapiens) existence, but these are outliers. Not everyone agrees with those dates.

Some will tell you that humans have existed for over 100,000 years. However, the creatures they refer to did not leave evidence of abstract thinking, complex language, written language, domesticated animals, cultivated crops, social civilizations, worship of deities, and more. So, what is it about those creatures that makes anyone believe they were true humans? The fact that a skeleton looks similar to a human skeleton does not make that creature a human or Homo sapiens.

About 5 thousand years ago, men started to make written records of historical events. We have written records from the Egyptians, the Chinese, the Sumerians, and others. These written records sometimes refer to people who lived a few thousand years before the dawn of writing and written records. They do not refer to humans living tens or hundreds of thousands of years ago, and definitely not millions of years before the time of those writings.

Using the genealogies given in the Bible, Bishop Ussher in the 16th and 17th centuries estimated the date for the creation of Adam at 4004 BC, or about 6 thousand years ago. Since then, other scholars have found that some of the genealogies in the Bible refer to grandfathers instead of fathers. Also, some generations seem to have been skipped, and there are other issues. They have determined that Adam, the first true human, was created about 6 thousand to as much as 10 thousand years ago.

Other scientific evidence from DNA studies and other methods finds that the date for the first true human is around 4000 to 8000 BC, or about 6 to 10 thousand years ago.

It seems that both Scripture and science have some range of possible dates for the first true humans, but both recognize a range of about 6 to 10 thousand years ago. So, **<u>Scripture and science tell the same story of origins (24).</u>**

So, what about those supposedly human remains that scientists find from much further back in history? While it may be unconventional thinking to much of the Judeo-Christian community today, the concept of very nearly human (hominin) creatures pre-dating Adam or coexisting with Adam is not a new concept. It has been accepted by Christians and Jews in the past, and there are Muslim sects that hold to that belief, as well as other pagan cultures (Egypt, India, China, etc.), which have had similar beliefs. Among Christians, the idea goes back at least as far as the 8th century.

Science says that true humans coexisted and may have mated with these pre-human, pre-Adamic creatures called hominin. One source I read says DNA mapping studies have found evidence of Neanderthal DNA among currently living humans. Science tells us that up to about 4 percent of modern human DNA is Neanderthal DNA. One theory says that Adam's body may have been supernaturally conceived by God in a hominin or pre-human female in much the same way as Jesus' body was supernaturally conceived by God in a human virgin. In First Corinthians 15:45, Paul refers to Jesus as the second Adam, and in Luke's genealogy of Jesus (Luke 3:38) he calls Adam the son of God. Do these suggest that Adam, like Jesus, was also supernaturally conceived by God in a virgin mother of a lower species? I do not know, but if I get to heaven and am told that Adam had a hominin mother, I am not going to say, "Excuse me, but I must be in the wrong city."

The whole subject of pre-Adamite people is controversial, but there may be some thin references to them in Scripture. There is the question of where Cain's wife came from, plus questions about who made up the population of the city Cain built. When God cursed Cain for killing his brother, He placed a mark on him so no one would kill him. Who existed to possibly kill him? The conventional explanation is that these were his siblings, but that is not clear from the Scriptures.

In Genesis 2:20a, the Scripture says that God brought all of the animals to Adam for him to name them. In the next phrase (Genesis 2:20b), it says no suitable mate was found for Adam. A common understanding is that Adam was looking for a mate among the animals he had just named. Was he really looking for a mate among dogs and cats and sheep and cows? Or is that second phrase a completely separate thought? Was he really looking for a mate among the hominin or near-human Neanderthal creatures with whom he lived?

Once again, I am not sure I totally agree with the idea of pre-Adamite populations, but scientific discoveries seem to indicate it is true, and I will keep an open mind on the subject. Is this a 31st point of agreement between Scripture and science? I just do not know, but it could be. I am not counting it for now.

Also note that the concept of pre-Adamic "people" has been around for a long time, but it has also been abused for a long time. It is a convenient excuse to identify a group one might despise as being non-human pre-Adamic people. Identifying them as non-human with no soul seems to justify mistreating them. If there are pre-Adamites who do not have the image of God, then they are simply animals and can be treated as such. It is a short step then to define a target group as descendants of pre-Adamites and justify treating them like animals… or worse.

Chapter 25:
Day seven - Rest

The Bible says that on the seventh day of creation God rested (Gen 2:2). The Bible never says that the seventh day has ended, so presumably the seventh day continues even today. Note that the first six days conclude with the phrase "there was evening and there was morning, the xth day." That phrase indicates that one day of creation ended and another began. However, day seven does not have that phrase, nor any other indication that it has ended. Do we think that is an oversight on God's part? I doubt that God forgot to include it. I can only conclude that day seven has not ended, which would mean that today we are still living in the seventh day of creation.

If God is resting today, does that mean He is asleep or totally disinterested in the course of His creation? When we think of rest, we think of sleep recharging our batteries because we have become tired. We need rest and sleep because we have the capability to become tired. If God is a God who never sleeps, obviously He needs no rest in the way we think of it. What Moses is saying is that God stopped creating new things. His creative work was complete. Just as when our work is complete, we rest, when God's creative work was complete, He rested. He stopped creating new materials, new forces, or new life forms. Resting is simply a way to say that the creation work was complete.

Science says humanity has been around for several thousand years, and while some new animal species may have been discovered, there is no evidence that they have not existed for even longer than humans have existed. In fact, while we have seen no new life forms appear, we have seen quite a few become extinct, even in our recent history. Today we have a list of creatures that are threatened with extinction, and we try to protect them. We have no list of creatures that exist today that did not exist for thousands of years. That is because God is resting from His creative works. If science has not found any new creatures living today that have not existed for over 10,000 years or longer than humans have existed, and if Scripture says that after God created Adam about 10,000 years ago, He stopped creating any new creatures, then **Scripture and science agree (28).**

We also see no new materials or elements appearing, no new basic forces or laws of physics appearing, and no new life forms appearing. Science says there is nothing new, and Scripture says God is resting and not creating anything new. In fact, the first verse of chapter 2 (Gen 2:1) says that the heavens and earth were finished at the end of day six. It also says repeatedly that it was good or very good (Gen 1:10, 12, 18, 21, 25, 31).

The fact that everything new appeared before the first humans and nothing new has appeared since tells us that something was in operation before the first humans that is no longer in operation today. We do not understand how the first life forms appeared or how the enormous complexity and diversity of life developed because it is no longer happening today, so we cannot observe and study it. The proliferation of new life forms stopped when God said it was finished at the end of day six, when the first human appeared.

So, what about the miracles recorded in the Scriptures? Did God create something new when He turned water into wine, fed 5,000 people with a few pieces of bread and fish, or made manna fall in the wilderness? In none of the miracles did God create any new materials or forces. He may have transformed one material into another, but He did not create any materials or forces that had never before existed. I suspect that the miracles in the Bible are supernatural applications of the laws of physics and chemistry that God created but that we do not yet understand.

There are intersections between the spirit realm and the physical realm. When the spirit realm affects something in the physical realm, we call it "supernatural." When God uses the spirit realm to intersect with the physical realm, it appears to be a miracle to us who are limited to the physical realm.

Consider that today we take for granted many things that people a few hundred years ago would have considered miracles. Think of electricity, indoor plumbing, telephones, movies, cell phones, GPS, television, and much more. We apply the principles of nature in ways the ancients could not have imagined. I expect that the miracles in the Bible are cases of God applying the forces of nature that He created in ways that even today we cannot imagine, so we call them supernatural.

This concept of rest is another area where Darwinism and Scripture continue to disagree. Darwinism says that the process of evolution is continuing even today. If that hypothesis is correct, we should be seeing a new creature or life form develop any day now. So far, no new creatures or life forms have been found. Maybe we should be seeing a superhuman evolve from a mere human. But we only see superhumans in cartoons and comic books.

While God is resting from His creative works, He is very active in the management of His creation. We see Him communicating with mankind. We have even seen Him become a man in the person of Jesus. You cannot get much more active than that.

If God rested from His creative works on the seventh day, and if He continues to rest from His creative works today, it seems reasonable to conclude that we are still in the seventh day of God's creation calendar. If we are still on the seventh day and have been in it for thousands of years, then how long is a creation day?

Also consider that the seventh day began only after Adam was created. So, day seven is effectively the era of human history. At this point, in chapter 2 of Genesis, the Bible narrative shifts from telling us about new things being created and begins to give us human history, including genealogies that we use to trace Adam's history or human history to approximately six to ten thousand years ago. Archaeologists tell us that we have about five thousand years of recorded human history, with some of those recorded stories telling us of human history before writing began. So, while science supports six to ten thousand years of time since Adam, it does not support a mere six geo-solar 24-hour earth days (144 hours) before Adam.

The seven-day pattern of six days of work followed by a day of rest is quite possibly given to us as a means for us to be constantly reminded that we are created beings. In the fourth of the Ten Commandments (Ex 20:8-11), God orders us to observe six days of labor plus a day of rest because God labored six days and rested one day during the creation of the universe. When we observe a seven-day week, we recognize that God is our creator. We recognize His authority to rule over us. This seven-day cycle with the implicit recognition of God's authority is so important to God that His prophets routinely condemned Israel for failure to observe it by keeping the seventh day set apart to worship God.

Challenge - Are you honoring God by faithfully observing a seven-day week and keeping one day set aside for worship?

American culture today largely ignores the command to keep every seventh day set aside to worship God. Sundays are for recreation and a variety of other activities that have nothing to do with rest or worship. We fail to recognize God as our creator with authority to require obedience, reverence, and respect from the creatures He created. If He judged Israel for profaning the Sabbath, how long will He be patient with us?

The seven-day pattern has also been considered by some scholars to be prophetic. When you apply the phrase "a day is as a thousand years" to the seven-day pattern of creation, you get six thousand years of human history followed by one thousand years of rest. The one thousand years, or millennium of human rest, is prophesied in many places in the Scriptures. If, as many people think, we are very near to the end of human history, some six thousand years after Adam, the pattern would fit nicely.

Chapter 26:
Fine-tuning

In many places, Scripture says that our universe, our world, and our bodies are wonderfully made. Scientists from many disciplines, including astronomy, physics, chemistry, geology, molecular biology, anthropology, and others, have been amazed at the fine-tuning they see in their field of study. They have even coined a term for this: the "anthropic" principle. The anthropic principle says the universe was uniquely designed for human existence. So, **Scripture and science agree (30)** that we live in a wonderful environment uniquely suited for human life.

It seems that the Earth and sun are unique among the planets and stars in their suitability to support life. In fact, there are hundreds, maybe thousands, of examples of fine tuning in the cosmos and the life sciences. The examples are too numerous to mention. Also, many of them involve a detailed understanding of the scientific discipline of the observer, which is far beyond my level of scientific understanding. However, let me give a few simple examples.

The force of gravity is just right to keep our solar system in balance and to keep our planet in the habitable zone of our Milky Way galaxy. If the force of gravity were a fraction of a fraction of a fraction of a percent higher or lower, it would make our earth uninhabitable. If it were too much, our earth would spiral into the sun. If it were too little, our earth would fly off into interstellar space.

The electrical charge on an electron is just right to make atoms possible. Again, if it were a tiny fraction of a percent too much or too little, atoms could not exist. The electrons that orbit the nucleus of an atom would either crash into the nucleus or fly off into space. With a little more or a little less, no atoms or elements could exist.

If the core of the earth did not have the exact amount of radioactive material, it would either fail to keep the core molten, preventing the formation of continents, or it would keep the core so hot that the surface of earth would be uninhabitable.

When scientists study the formation of solar systems throughout the universe, they find that the physics of the natural process makes it almost impossible for a rocky planet like earth to form in the Goldilocks Zone—not too cold and not too hot—around its central star. Our solar system seems to have been uniquely created, with Earth placed just the right distance from the sun. Too close or too far away would make life impossible.

I once watched a Science Channel program on the origins of our solar system and our planet. In a one-hour program, they used some variation of the term "lucky" so many times that I lost count. They seemed to recognize that our home planet is special because of a series of very unique events during its formation. They called it luck, but I call it divine design.

I also have a few books that list a number of examples of precision in molecular biology, but I do not understand them well enough to summarize them accurately. However, the PhDs who authored those books considered those features to be too precise to have happened by "accident."

The uniqueness even extends to the exact chemistry and physics of the elements. If oxygen, nitrogen, carbon, hydrogen, and other elements did not have the exact features that they do have, our existence would not be possible. The ways these elements uniquely form our environment are the subject of an entire book on my bookshelf.

Regardless of the scientific discipline, there are many physical constants that sit on a razor's edge of precision. To get one or two of these features to be so precise might have happened by accident, but to get hundreds of features to be so precise could not have been an accident. It must have had a design, which means it must have had an intelligent designer and a skilled builder.

In Scripture, there is the general sense that earth was uniquely made to be a habitation for mankind. This is repeated in many passages. In Scripture, there is also the comment during Day One of creation that says the Spirit of God hovered over the early universe (Gen 1:2a). Presumably, this means God was managing the development of all these very precise physical features.

Chapter 27:
Scripture – science parallels

Following is a list of my 30 points of agreement or parallels between the story of creation in scripture and the findings of science relative to origins.

	Science says	Scripture says
1	There was a beginning	There was a beginning
2	Original singularity of pure raw energy, the size of a single atom	God made that which is seen from that which is not seen
3	The universe inflated	God stretched out the heavens
4	Original state was a shapeless cloud of sub-atomic particles. No structure and no materials.	Original state without form and void
5	Original matter in a fluid quantum state. Dirac sea.	The Spirit of God hovered over the "waters"
6	EMF appeared after sub-atomic particles, and the strong nuclear force appeared	God said Let there be light after the quantum state of matter

7	Electromagnetic force (light) makes atoms possible	No mention of physical matter (atoms) until after light was created
8	No gravity in the early part of the inflation	Gravity not created until "Day 2"
9	After simple atoms are formed, the weak nuclear force causes fusion reactions inside stars, which form heavy elements	On day 3, God made heavy elements that make up rocks (land) and water
10	Weak nuclear force causes radioactive decay of heavy elements in Earth's core, which keeps Earth's core molten, causing tectonic forces that raise continents	God separated dry land and oceans on day 3
11	First life to appear was plant life	First life to appear was plant life
12	All physical materials and forces were completed before the first life appeared	God created land, seas, time, and space before the first life was created
13	There has been a progression in the appearance of new features and creatures	God created new features in a progression of events over a period of 6 "days".

14	Solar system & planet Earth appeared 9 billion years after physical materials and forces were completed in the beginning	God set the solar system in place and synchronized their motions on "day 4"
15	Time dilation makes time pass at different rates for persons with different perspectives	With God, a day is as a thousand years and a thousand years is as a day
16	Spontaneous generation of life by totally natural forces is impossible	God supernaturally created the first life
17	The first animal life was marine life, which reproduces by laying eggs	On day 5, God created marine life as the first animal life
18	After marine life came birds, which also reproduce by laying eggs	On day 5, God created flying life (birds)
19	All egg-laying life forms appeared "suddenly" during the Cambrian explosion of new life. No precedents.	God created egg-laying creatures on Day 5 .... not before & not after
20	No new egg-laying creatures since the Cambrian explosion	Day 5 was completed. God said it is good
21	Mammal (birthing) life forms exploded into being	God created land life (birthing creatures) on day

	after egg-laying life forms had matured and gone through several extinction events	six …. Not before & not after
22	Science says DNA mutations do not generate new families/kinds	God commanded animals to reproduce after their own kinds
23	Humans are the last life form to appear on Earth	God created man on Day 6 after creating other birthing creatures
24	The first true humans appeared only about 10,000 years ago. About 5,000 years of recorded human history	Adam was created about 6,000 to 10,000 years ago
25	Humans are the highest life form in terms of capability for complex language and abstract thinking	Adam named the creatures – indicates language and abstract thinking
26	Humans are the only creatures that show any desire to worship a creator	Man is the only creature created in the image of God. Adam talked to God in the Garden of Eden
27	Out-of-body and near-death experiences indicate that man has a consciousness apart from the body	Man was created in the image of God with an eternal soul/spirit

28	No new life forms have been discovered that have not existed since before man existed.	Creation is complete – God rested from His creative works on day 7
29	The sequence of origins is inanimate materials, then plants, then sea life, then birds, then land animals, then man	The sequence of creation is inanimate materials, then plants, then sea life, then birds, then land animals, then man
30	Many scientific disciplines recognize the extreme fine-tuning of features that make planet Earth uniquely suited as a home for life.	In many places, Scripture says that our earth is wonderfully made.

So far, I have identified 30 instances where Scripture and science agree on the subject of origins. Having 30 points that could agree or not agree, but which all happen to agree, is like flipping 30 coins and having all 30 land "heads." Basic statistical calculations find that the odds against that happening naturally or accidentally are over 1 billion to one. Therefore, the odds against the Biblical stories of creation and the scientific stories of origins being different stories are over 1 billion to one. The simple odds are over 1 billion to one that **<u>Scripture and science tell the same story of origins.</u>** This is far beyond the realm of coincidence. It is far beyond the possibility that the writers of the Bible could have accidentally drafted a story that science would confirm to such a high degree thousands of years later. The story of creation in Scripture must have been inspired by the Creator. Those odds indicate that the creation story is scientifically accurate, not a myth, and that the Creator God is a real person, not a myth.

Note: Even if you challenge or disallow six or seven of my points of agreement between Scripture and science, the odds remain very high that the story told by Scripture and the story told by science are the same story. With only 20 points of agreement, the statistical odds are still over 1 million to one that the two stories are the same.

This remarkable level of agreement raises a question. Most of the Scripture regarding creation was written by Moses about 3,300 years ago, more than 3,000 years before any of the modern science was discovered. The most recent writings in Scripture were completed almost 2,000 years ago. Whether 2,000 or 3,000 years ago, how did Moses and the other authors know these things if the Creator God did not reveal them?

I should probably insert a note here about perceived inconsistencies in the Biblical account of creation. When you try to pick apart the Genesis account and analyze it, you find that it is not as complete an account as inquiring minds might prefer. There are many questions we can ask that the account does not answer. Does this mean the account is any less true? If I tell you that this morning I got out of bed at 6:00 a.m., took a shower, brushed my teeth, ate breakfast, went to work, came home, ate dinner, and went to bed at 10:00 p.m., is my account any less true because I did not tell you what I did at work or what I ate at every meal? If later I tell you that I ate a meal at noon, can you say that this is an inconsistency in my story because my earlier account said I was at work all day?

In chapter 1 of Genesis, we read an account of creation, and in chapter 2, we read a further account that adds details. On the surface, there seems to be some disagreement between the two accounts. For example, chapter 1 says that plants were created first, before man, but chapter 2 seems to say that man was created before any shrub of the field had appeared on the earth. Critics seize upon these apparent contradictions to claim that the Bible is an unreliable book filled with errors, and therefore must not be true. However, is it not possible that the two accounts are both true and that we simply do not have enough information in a few hundred words to know every detail about everything that happened in the exact sequence in which it happened? You also need to understand that chapter 2 is not about original creation, but about human history after the original creation. The two accounts are telling different stories.

The bottom line is that, regardless of the exact sequence of each detail, the exact elapsed time, or the exact process, the design and the energy for a universe of incredible complexity and precision—made from seventeen subatomic particles and four basic forces—along with the design and energy behind the first material beings with life, came from the one and only omnipotent, omniscient, eternal being that we call God. The exact process and detailed timeline God used may not be fully understood, but there was nothing random or accidental about it. We are completely rational and justified in believing that every word of the account of creation in the Bible is true, even if we do not completely understand all of the implications of some of those words.

Chapter 28:
So what?

The operative question becomes, So what? So, what if the story of creation in Scripture is technically, scientifically, and historically verifiable as true and accurate? So what if I believe that there is a Creator God who created the universe and all life? Why does it matter?

In society, it matters because it affects our worldview. Darwinism, with its concepts of man as a mere animal and survival of the fittest, when embraced to its fullest measure, has led to extreme racism, ethnic cleansing, and other evils. The Nazis used this ideological belief to justify the slaughter of millions of persons whom they considered not fit to survive. Hitler, Mussolini, Stalin, Lenin, Mao, Pol Pot, and others also slaughtered millions of people and were heavily influenced by Darwinian philosophies. Logical progressions of the concept of man as just another animal and survival of the fittest lead to acceptance of euthanasia, abortion, infanticide, and ethnic cleansing, among other evils. The proponents of Darwinism or evolution fail to mention this unpleasant and inconvenient historical fact.

Closer to home, Darwinism and atheism, which reject God and focus on personal satisfaction, result in widespread immoral and unethical behaviors. Lying, cheating, stealing, promiscuity, homosexuality, gender dysphoria, greed, violence, selfishness, and more are natural results of rejecting the teachings of the Creator God. When you teach several generations of youth that they are mere animals responsible to no God and no supreme authority, you should not be surprised when they act like animals.

On the personal level, if you believe that there is a Creator God, it stands to reason that He and He alone has the supreme moral and legal authority to establish the rules of behavior for His creation. As Creator, He makes the rules and sets rewards and penalties for conformance to those rules. These rules tell us how to achieve the optimum performance and satisfaction we were designed for. Therefore, if the Creator God has given us the Scriptures as an operator's manual for the human spirit, it makes logical sense to study and apply those principles to our lives.

When you believe that the Creator God is real and that He created us in His image with an eternal soul, it will affect your priorities. We spend a lot of attention and effort on our physical health. We exercise, we are careful about what we consume, we practice good hygiene, and so on. All this is done in an effort to maintain good physical health for ourselves and our families. While this is all good, it merely has a temporal impact on our total well-being. At the end of our life on earth, it all turns to dust.

On the other hand, when we recognize that our spiritual health has an eternal impact rather than a temporal one, we will prioritize activities that improve our spiritual health. We will be careful about what we put into our minds through social media, television, books, and other sources. We will make a habit of reading God's Word. We will spend time with godly people. We will faithfully attend church. We will follow the instructions in the "owner's manual," the Bible. In short, we will be very serious about our spiritual health and the spiritual health of our family.

When you truly understand that our God is the Creator of the universe and everything in it, you develop a sense of awe for the God who could speak and make that happen. A sense of awe is necessary for true worship. Without it, any attempt at worship tends to be shallow.

The Creator God is real. He is a real person, not a myth or a fictional character like Santa Claus or the Easter Bunny. He is a real person with the power, the intellect, the will, and the time to create the universe and all life forms. He is the very definition of righteousness and holiness. He is not someone to be trifled with or ignored. He is the Creator, whether you choose to believe it or not.

If you choose to believe any of the usual interpretations of the creation story—whether six days, gap, apparent age, or others—and if your faith is solid and unwavering in that concept, do not let anything I have written dissuade you from your belief in a Creator God and the truth of His Word.

However, if you accept that some of the observations of the scientific community are accurate, true, and valid, and if that challenges your faith, then I want you to know there is a valid scriptural interpretation of Genesis that can be totally consistent with the factual evidence (not speculative theories) that science has discovered about the origins of nature, God's creation.

So, whether you choose to believe God created everything in a mature state over a period of six rotations of planet Earth about six thousand years ago, or whether you choose to believe God created everything in six creative episodes, each with a duration suitable to the workday of a timeless eternal Creator, it is vitally important for you to be fully convinced that there is a God, that we have been created by that God, and that He alone is worthy of our ultimate respect, reverence, and obedience.

As I have said, the "who" of creation is critical to believe. The "what, where, when, and how" of the creation mechanics are interesting but secondary in importance. There is room for differences in those areas, but no room for difference of belief in the "who" of creation.

Chapter 29:
Making disciples

Whether you are a skeptic yourself or you are trying to win a skeptic to Christ, at some point you will likely have to deal with the truth about creation. Most of our culture today has been deeply indoctrinated in the concept of Darwinian evolution, which is often misrepresented as settled truth. If you believe in a Creator God, they may call you a knuckle-dragger, a flat-earther, and other ugly names. Getting past that paradigm is a real challenge.

One of my big problems with the young earth creation (YEC) folks is this. For about 100 years, our public schools have taught that the development of our world and its life forms has spanned millions or even billions of years. Whether you believe in natural evolution or divine creation, the plain fact is that the natural universe God created contains a lot of convincing evidence for a timeline much longer than the YEC position allows.

With the YEC reading of six 24-hour days of creation standing in stark contrast to clear evidence from multiple scientific disciplines showing billions of years of history, many people conclude that the story of creation in the Bible is a myth. If they believe that the creation story is a myth, then the rest of the Bible becomes suspect, and the existence of a Creator God is no more real to them than Zeus, Jupiter, Poseidon, Thor, or any of the ancient mythological gods.

In the New Testament book of Hebrews (Hebrews 11:6), Paul says that in order for a man to seek after God, he must first believe that God exists. While that sounds like a "well, of course" kind of statement, it is important enough to be included in Scripture. The first hurdle to winning a major portion of our world today to Christ is to convince them that the Creator God is not a myth. Convince them that He is real. Convince them that He exists. As long as they believe that creation is a myth and the Creator God is a myth, they have no reason to seek a relationship with that Creator God.

For those folks, a creation story with six geosolar earth days only about 6,000 years ago is a major barrier to belief in a Creator God. That being the case, the evangelist has two choices. First, he can try to convince them that all of the evidence collected in the past few hundred years by astronomers, geologists, anthropologists, physicists, and others from all over the world is totally wrong about the age of the universe, planet Earth, and life itself. Good luck with that one.

The second choice for an evangelist is to convince people that the word "day" in Scripture can mean something other than 24 hours. The evidence supporting billions of years is strong. The evidence supporting 24-hour days is debatable at best.

I have read statements by prominent YEC advocates that effectively say you cannot be a Christian if you do not believe in a young earth creation. This makes the barrier to faith both high and wide. In Matthew 23:13, Mark 9:24, and Luke 11:52, Jesus condemned the Pharisees for creating unnecessary barriers for those seeking God. Again, in 1 Corinthians 8:9, He warns against being a stumbling block to those who are weak. I suspect that the dogmatic YEC "six-day" ideology probably falls into that same category of barriers.

When I was eight years old, I accepted Christ as my Lord and King. I trusted Him to save me from a life of sin and misery and to save me from an eternity of torment. I believed then, and I believe now, that this is the simple message of the gospel. Nothing needs to be added. Faith in Christ alone is sufficient for my salvation. What I believe about the lengths of the days of creation is immaterial as long as I completely trust the "who" of creation. The "how" and the "when" of creation are interesting to know, but they only affect my salvation if they influence what I believe about the "who" of creation.

In other words, what I believe about the length of the days in Genesis does not affect my relationship with God or my salvation. I can be a faithful Christian and believe either YEC or OEC. On the other hand, if I am telling a friend about Jesus and they are reluctant to accept Him as God because of the perception that the Bible is a myth, then an "allegorical" OEC interpretation of the days in Genesis can be a valuable tool to break down that barrier and build a bridge to faith.

Chapter 30:
Death & Rebirth

A third monster in the room when discussing Biblical creation is the subject of death.

A common understanding of the punishment of Adam and Eve after they ate the forbidden fruit is that they were condemned to physically die. In fact, many teach that all of the animal world was condemned to physical death due to Adam and Eve's disobedience. Presumably, this means that every life form—mammals, fish, birds, insects, bacteria, etc.—had eternal life until Adam and Eve sinned. It is not clear if these folks believe that plants are included in that curse or if plants could die before the curse. If plants were included in that curse, and if they had eternal life before the curse, then no animal could eat anything since plants are the base of the food chain for all life. If plants were not included in that curse, why not?

The young earth creationists have a train of logic which seems to say that nothing died physically for the first six days. No bacteria died, no insects died, no plants died, no animals died, and so on. If this is true, then no animals were able to eat anything. No lions ate any dead zebras, no cattle ate any dead vegetation, and so on. Therefore, they argue that the six days had to be very short days, or everything would have starved. It seems that their train of logic has a questionable base assumption. The whole of creation may have happened in six days of 24 hours (I do not think so, but it is possible), but this issue of death does not prove that to be true. I think that those who use the introduction of death as proof for a young earth are on shaky ground.

The conventional wisdom among many Christians is that decay and physical death entered the world, and indeed the universe, when Adam sinned. One thing they point to is the fact that God declared His creation to be "good" on several occasions during the six days of creation, and they refuse to believe that God could declare anything that included physical death to be good. That seems to be a very human perspective.

These folks seem to read God's mind and assign to Him a character they have made up, a character just as offended by physical death as mortals are. It is almost as though they create an idol, a god of their own making. According to them, God created a death-free world, which was ruined by sin. However, in truth, if God created a physical life cycle of birth, growth, maturity, and death, He could call it good from His perspective even if there was physical death. If there were no sin, it would be good from God's perspective. Once sin entered creation, it would be cursed. Furthermore, since only man is capable of sin, the curse would apply only to humans.

It is important to recognize that death was the penalty for sin. Humans are the only creatures with the capability to sin against God. Animals do not have the ability to sin; they always behave according to the natural instincts that God programmed into them at creation. Since animals cannot sin, they need not be cursed because of sin. The curse of death applied only to humans.

Another point to consider is that if there was no death in the world, then God's warning to Adam that he would die if he ate of the forbidden fruit would have had no meaning to an Adam who did not know what death was. When God warned Adam against eating the forbidden fruit, He said that on the day he ate of it, he would surely die (Gen 2:17). If there had never been any death of any kind, how would Adam have known the consequences of disobedience? The warning would have had no meaning to Adam. For the warning to have any meaning, he surely would have been aware of what death is. Adam never asked God, "What do you mean by die?"

Also, if the penalty for eating the forbidden fruit was physical death, then it took several hundred years for that sentence to be imposed. Consider the story carefully. God told Adam that on the day he ate of the forbidden fruit he would surely die (Gen 2:17). Adam did not immediately die physically when he ate the fruit. He lived for over nine hundred years (Gen 5:5) and had many sons and daughters.

On the other hand, Adam did immediately die spiritually. As soon as they ate the fruit, Adam and Eve died spiritually. Instead of walking with God in the garden as they had been doing, they hid themselves and covered their bodies with fig leaves (Gen 3:7-9). They no longer had the close fellowship with God that they had enjoyed previously. They became separated from God and spiritually "dead." Note again that since animals were not created in the image of God, they have no soul or spirit that can be separated from God in a spiritual death. If the curse of death is a spiritual death, it cannot apply to animals, only to humans.

Now, fast forward about 4000 years to Jesus's conversation with Nicodemus. Jesus told him that to have eternal life he must be born again (John 3:3), not born again physically but born of the spirit. Since we are all born spiritually dead due to Adam's sin, we must be born of the spirit to restore the original created condition of fellowship with God (John 3:6). It seems that the human spirit which died in the garden needs to be reborn by consciously accepting Jesus as our King, our Lord, our God, and our ultimate authority in all things. The part of Adam that died in the garden must be born again to reestablish a relationship with God. Once again, that sounds like the death that entered the world in the garden was a spiritual death, not a physical death.

The Scriptural narrative tells us that because of Adam's disobedience we are all born spiritually dead, and if we do not remedy that condition by accepting Jesus before we physically die, we will be eternally spiritually dead, which means eternally separated from God. On the other hand, if we accept Jesus as our God and King before we physically die, He gives us a new birth, makes us spiritually alive, ends the separation from God, and reestablishes the relationship that Adam originally had with God in the garden.

So, since Adam died spiritually and all his descendants were born as spiritually dead sinners, we all need to be born again, born of the spirit, in order to have fellowship and communion with the Creator God. How do we get this new birth? The only way is to accept Jesus Christ as our God, our King, our Lord, and our ultimate authority in all things. When we accept Him and follow and obey Him, we can trust Him to make us spiritually alive and save us from a life of misery and an eternity of torment.

Epilogue/challenge

The evidence for an eternal, super-intelligent, super-powerful creator God is abundant. As creator, this God has supreme authority. He is the King. He gets to set the rules.

The first humans disobeyed His rules, causing Him great disappointment, sorrow, and grief. His holy and righteous justice demanded that He impose the penalty of spiritual death, or separation from God, on the human creatures He loved and on all their descendants, which includes us. Remember that while God is a loving God, His overriding primary characteristic is holiness. His holiness does not allow Him to fellowship with sin. Sinners must be separated from God, which is the definition of spiritual death.

God's love drove Him to pay the penalty for our disobedience and sin by becoming a man, living a sinless life, and sacrificing His life on a cross to give each of us the opportunity to be forgiven and made whole again.

The price of obtaining that forgiveness is to acknowledge His Son Jesus as the King that He is and to accept Him as your personal King. Christians describe this acceptance in different ways: surrender to Christ, invite Him into your heart, accept Him as your Savior, believe in Jesus, follow Jesus, and more. All of these are ways to say that you accept Jesus as your ultimate and absolute authority in all things and commit yourself to love and serve Him, living your life according to His instructions.

When we acknowledge our status as sinners, and when we sincerely and totally accept Him as our King, we can confidently trust Him to give us a new birth, a spiritual birth that makes us spiritually alive. We can trust Him to save us from a life of misery, hopelessness, disillusionment, and disappointment, and to give us a life of peace, joy, and hope. We can trust Him to save us from an eternity of torment and give us an eternal home beyond our wildest dreams. We can trust God to be a loving heavenly Father.

If you are offended by the concept of accepting Jesus as your King, ask yourself a question: if Heaven is Christ's kingdom, as is taught in Scripture, how many people would you expect to find in Heaven who reject Jesus as King? I dare say that if you do not accept Him as King, you have no place in His kingdom. Is there a happy medium between total acceptance and total rejection? The answer is clearly no. I call Heaven "barbed wire country." You cannot sit on the fence in barbed wire country. You must be totally on one side or the other. You either accept Jesus totally or reject Him. You have to make a conscious decision to accept Him. The default position of no acceptance is rejection.

It is important to note that Jesus Christ, the creator God, is the only Supreme God. There are not many ways to approach God; there is only one way. Some people teach that all faiths lead to God. The problem is that most of those faiths are mutually exclusive. The only way to have a relationship with the one true God is through acceptance of Jesus Christ.

The conclusion is this: there is a creator God. There is only one true God. He did create you. What are you going to do about it? Will you accept Him, accept His way, obey Him, and serve Him, or will you reject Him and His way, and try to live life your own way? As Joshua told the Israelites, "Choose you this day whom you will serve" (Joshua 24:15). If you have never accepted Jesus as your King, I urge you to do it today. You will never regret it, not now and not hereafter.

Appendix 1: Select Bibliography - Good books I recommend for further reading/study

In recent years, perhaps 30 or 40 years, there have been many books published on the subject of creation. If you search Amazon for books on creation, you will get a lot of results. I have read more than 60 of them. Following is a list of some that I have found to be very helpful.

<u>Books I have read and recommend for further study:</u>

Creation: Remarkable Evidence of God's Design, Grant R. Jeffrey, WaterBrook Press, 2003

Information: The Key to Life, Werner Gitt, Master Books, 2023

Signature in the Cell: DNA and the Evidence for Intelligent Design, Stephen C. Meyer, HarperCollins, 2010

Darwin Devolves, Michael J. Behe, HarperOne, 2020

The Creator and the Cosmos: How the Latest Scientific Discoveries Reveal God, Hugh Ross, RTB Press, 2018

The Quantum Genesis, Alessandro Candeas, …….

Quantum Genesis, Stuart Allen, Deep River Books, 2018

The Edge of Evolution, Michael J. Behe, Free Press, 2008

The Galileo Connection, Charles E. Hummel, IVP Books, 1986

Darwin's Doubt, Stephen C. Meyer, HarperOne, 2013

A Mousetrap for Darwin, Michael J. Behe, Discovery Institute Press, 2020

The Fingerprint of God, Hugh Ross, Promise Publishing, 1989

Navigating Genesis, Hugh Ross, RTB Press, 2014

Designed to the Core, Hugh Ross, RTB Press, 2022

More Than a Theory, Hugh Ross, Baker Books, 2009

Why the Universe Is the Way It Is, Hugh Ross, Baker Books, 2008

Improbable Planet, Hugh Ross, Baker Books, 2016

Heaven Is Beyond Imagination, Jacques LaFrance, Kindle Direct Publishing, 2021

Darwin's Black Box, Michael J. Behe, Free Press Publishing, 2006

Return of the God Hypothesis, Stephen C. Meyer, HarperOne, 2021

Evolution: Still a Theory in Crisis, Michael Denton, Discovery Institute Press, 2016

Creation, Evolution, and Intelligent Design, J. B. Stump / Ken Ham / Hugh Ross / Deborah Haarsma / Stephen Meyer, Zondervan, 2017

Foresight, Marcos Eberlin, Discovery Institute Press, 2019

The Miracle of Man, Michael Denton, Discovery Institute Press, 2019

A Matter of Days: Resolving a Creation Controversy, Hugh Ross, RTB Press, 2015

Genesis and the Big Bang, Gerald R. Schroeder, Bantam Books, 2011

Creation and the Big Bang, Clare Raynard Magoon, WestBow Press, 2018

Old Earth or Evolutionary Creation, Kenneth Keathley / J. B. Stump / Joe Aguirre / et al., InterVarsity Press, 2017

Understanding Intelligent Design: Everything You Need to Know in Plain Language, William Dembski & Sean McDowell, Harvest House Publications, 2008

The New Creationism: Building Scientific Theory on a Biblical Foundation, Paul Garner, Evangelical Press, 2017

A Biblical Case for an Old Earth, David Snoke, Baker Books, 2006

In Six Days, John F. Ashton, Master Books, 2001

Divine Engineering, David N. Breams, InterVarsity Press, 2018

The Creator Revealed, Michael G. Strauss, WestBow Press, 2018

Genesis One and the Origin of Earth, Newman / Phillips / Eckelmann, Interdisciplinary Biblical Research Institute, 2007

Coming to Peace with Science, Darrel R. Falk, IVP Academic, 2004

Mystery of Life's Origin, Thaxton / Bradley / Olsen / Tour / Meyer / Wells / Gonzales / Miller / Klinghoffer, Discovery Institute Press, 2020

Evolution and Intelligent Design in a Nutshell, Lo / Chien / Anderson / Alston / Waltzer, Discovery Institute Press, 2020

The Science of God, Gerald L. Schroeder, Free Press, 1997

Friend of Science, Friend of Faith, Gregg Davidson, Kregel Publications, 2019

Some of these are pretty easy reading for the average person, but some are deeply technical and might be a bit of a yawner for many folks. I have various degrees of agreement with these authors, but they are all thought-provoking, which is a good thing. They have all influenced my thinking on creation.

Also, some of these books have bibliographies of their own with more suggestions for good books on creation. Mine is not even close to an exhaustive list of good books on creation versus science.

Most of these books focus on showing how evolution by materialistic natural "accidental" causes, or Darwinism, is facing increasing challenges from scientists. At this point, it is very difficult for objective scientists to support the Darwinian concept of origins. They are left with divine creation or Intelligent Design (ID) as the only alternatives. One of the above books contains several dozen quotes by prominent scientists stating that evolution is scientifically impossible and can only be accepted by atheistic "faith."

What I have found lacking in most publications on the subject is a focus on showing that the blow-by-blow or verse-by-verse account of creation in Scripture is scientifically and historically true and accurate. They typically show that divine creation is the best choice, but they fail to show that the narrative of creation in the Bible is a true and accurate story of the origins of the universe and all life in it.

So, I decided to write my own book. In 2018, I published Moses and the Big Bang, which suggests that God revealed the Big Bang to Moses some 3,300 years ago. In my naivete about the publishing business, I thought that if I paid a publishing company (commonly called self-publishing or vanity publishing) to put the book into print and have it listed on the websites of major booksellers, then people would find it and buy it. Also, my naivete about writing meant it was not a well-written book. I quickly learned that you need to actively market a book to sell it, and marketing books is not a skill set that old diesel engine engineers possess. Hopefully, I will do better this time.

Appendix 2: Moses as author of Genesis

Tradition tells us that Genesis, the first book of the Bible, was written by Moses. Despite efforts by some scholars to prove multiple authors, there is no widely accepted proof to challenge the tradition.

Genesis traces the formation of the Hebrew nation from the time of the first man until the birth of the nation. Moses himself tells us that he was a Hebrew baby who was adopted by an Egyptian princess and raised as an Egyptian prince until about the age of forty.

As an Egyptian prince, he would have been educated in all the knowledge of Egypt. Since Egypt was a world power and a center of learning, we can assume that he had at his disposal all the literary, political, religious, engineering, and scientific knowledge available in the world at that time. The scientific understanding of the Egyptians would have been rudimentary by today's standards, and the scientific understanding of the common person in the nation of Israel for whom Genesis was written would have been even more limited.

That is not to say that they were ignorant or less intellectually evolved than we are today. They knew enough to build chariots, irrigation works, houses, temples, and other imposing structures. It is simply to say that the collective scientific knowledge of mankind then was less than today, and the tools required to study fine details were not yet developed. By the way, most high school graduates today could not build a working chariot or an irrigation system if they had to.

As with most ancient cultures, Moses would have been familiar with the movements of the stars. However, this would have been limited to the movements he could see with the naked eye, since telescopes were not invented until thousands of years later.

As a prince of Egypt, Moses would have been literate and familiar with many languages. He almost certainly would have read almost everything available at the time and was undoubtedly familiar with many literary styles. In fact, in Acts 7:22, Dr. Luke said Moses was educated in all the wisdom of Egypt and was mighty in words.

So, the account of Genesis in the Bible was written in the Hebrew language as spoken in Moses's day. Some see the account in Genesis as having been written in the form of a chiastic poem, where thoughts are repeated in reverse order for emphasis. It might also have included literary styles from other languages of that day. Linguists believe they understand the exact meaning of each word and phrase. However, languages evolve over time, and idioms may have existed that are no longer understood.

Also, consider that it is likely Moses did not "write" the words himself but dictated them to scribes. Today, we think of writing as typing on a computer keyboard. Writing on papyrus scrolls was tedious and time-consuming. It was probably dictated in small "batches" over months or years and perhaps to various scribes writing different sections. However, Moses was the human author inspired by the divine author in that the ideas and principles came from or through him. Some experts see slight differences in style for various sections and try to use that to discredit the idea of Moses as the author. These differences do not necessarily disprove the authorship of Moses.

For the purposes of this book, we are sticking with over 3,000 years of tradition stating that Moses is the author of *Genesis*.

Appendix 3: Apologetics/proofs of scripture

The fact that the story of creation in the Bible is supported to such a high degree by the findings of scientists is only one of many proofs of the veracity of the Holy Scriptures. The following are a few of those other areas of proof. Many good books have already been written about each of these, so I will only mention them briefly.

The story of all but a very few humans being destroyed by a major catastrophic flood is also supported by the findings of scientists. While there may be some debate about whether the flood of Noah was universal in terms of geography or universal in terms of humanity, there is abundant geological evidence for a major flood. There is also abundant evidence in DNA studies to conclude that all humans today descended from a very small group of ancestors about 5,000 years ago. Presumably, we all came from the eight persons on Noah's ark.

There are many prophecies that have been fulfilled in great detail. Perhaps one of the most impressive is a prophecy regarding the date of Christ's triumphal entry into Jerusalem. It was fulfilled on that precise date even though it was prophesied hundreds of years earlier. Only the God who created time could have inspired those prophecies in such detail.

Archaeology often finds evidence of historical facts mentioned in the Bible. My favorite is the fact that while the Bible mentions the Hittite peoples several times, for hundreds of years scholars claimed that there had never been any Hittite culture, let alone one that was a major power. Then, archaeologists discovered the capital city of the Hittite empire, confirming the record of the Bible. Again, this is only one of many such confirmations of the biblical record of history.

Proofs of the life, death, and resurrection of Jesus are abundant. People have tried for centuries to dismiss Jesus as simply a backwater prophet and deny his resurrection, but the facts always confirm the story in the Bible. He was crucified and He did rise again.

Possibly one of the most impressive proofs is the record of the preservation of Scripture. Men have tried to wipe out the Bible many times, but it always survives. Not only that, but the accuracy of its preservation is astounding. Compared to other ancient writings, we have biblical manuscripts dated closer to the original writings than we have for any other ancient texts. Our current versions of the Bible have few, if any, errors compared to those near-original manuscripts.

Each of the above areas of proof has volumes written about them. Each is an interesting study. The bottom line is that the Bible is a reliable word from the Creator God to His created beings. It is worth your effort to study the whole volume in depth and apply its principles to your life.

Appendix 4: The spirit realm

In the beginning God created the heavens and the earth. I have expressed the idea that the "heavens" refer to the spirit realm. What do I mean by that? In our culture, we talk about angels and demons without really thinking about them much or knowing much about them. The Bible tells us about a number of beings that populate the spirit realm. We tend to lump them all together as angels, but there are archangels, cherubim, seraphs, demons, and other angelic creatures who do not have physical bodies such as we do. Their bodies are not composed of atoms and molecules, or "the dust of the earth." They have spirit bodies.

These spirit beings exist in an environment that is not well known to us. We talk a lot about heaven and hell, but we really do not know much about either of them. The Bible also tells us about different levels of heaven. In 2 Corinthians 12:2, Paul says he knows a man who was caught up into the third heaven and saw things that cannot be uttered. The term translated "heavens" can mean one of three things. First, it can mean the Earth's atmosphere where clouds form and birds fly. Second, it can mean the universe where stars, galaxies, and other objects exist. Third, it can mean the spirit realm where angels live.

People who have had near-death experiences tell of visiting a realm that has a variety of amazing features and is populated by the spirits of people who have died, plus angelic beings. Like the physical realm, the spirit realm exists. It is real.

All of these angelic creatures and their environment were created. The angels have not existed since eternity past, so at some point they had a beginning. The heavenly environment where these spirit creatures exist also had a beginning. Verse one of Genesis tells us that the heavenly realm, or spirit realm, where all those angels and other spirit creatures exist, was created by the same God who created our physical universe. Those creatures are created beings and not worthy of worship. Only the Creator God is worthy of worship.

Except for the first verse, the story of creation in the Bible tells us only about the creation of the physical realm. The first verse tells us that both the spirit realm and the physical realm were created by the same God. The Bible goes on to tell us about the creation of the physical realm but never tells us any details about the creation of the spirit realm. Presumably, the details of the creation of the spirit realm are beyond human ability to comprehend. All we need to know is that God created that spirit realm as well as our more familiar physical realm.

About the Author

Ken Goss was born in Savanna, Illinois, to parents of modest means who loved the Lord and their family. He attended public high school in Mt. Carroll, Illinois. He then earned an engineering degree from LeTourneau College in Longview, Texas, followed by an MBA from the University of Detroit.

Ken grew up faithfully attending an independent, fundamental Bible church. He accepted Jesus Christ as his Lord and King at age eight. Having trusted Christ to save him from a life of misery and an eternity of torment, Ken became a lifelong student of the Bible and an active church member. While an engineering student at LeTourneau College, he chose all his liberal arts electives from the Bible curriculum. At LeTourneau, he also attended years of daily chapel services with many excellent guest lecturers. Added to this base of formal study have been years of sitting in pews, along with independent personal studies.

Ken has spent more than forty years as an engineer in the auto industry. Job assignments required frequent travel between Michigan and places such as Brazil, Italy, Austria, and Germany. On work assignments, he has also visited Mexico, Korea, Taiwan, France, Spain, Poland, England, the Netherlands, Switzerland, and Belgium. He spent three years living in Brazil on assignment. He has spoken Portuguese and Italian at modest levels of proficiency.

Job-related moves have resulted in home church changes, so he and his family have fellowshipped with Baptists, Nazarenes, Brethren, Methodists, Presbyterians, and other fundamental Bible or community churches. He has served in leadership positions in some of those home churches.

He is married to his high school sweetheart, and together they cherish four children and eleven grandchildren. Ken chose to invest significantly in tuition to send his four children to thirteen years each of Christian schools, primarily so they would understand that they are created beings with a responsibility to their Creator. Ken also served on some of those school boards for several years.

Ken is now retired from engineering and makes his home in Clarkston, Michigan.